THE EAGLE SIGNAL

The Eagle Signal

Dr. Jeannie Frazier

Seymour Books

Published by Seymour Books

ISBN 978-1-7256-1857-2

Typesetting services by BOOKOW.COM

I want to dedicate this book to my late parents:
Robert C. Frazier and Epsy Anne Holloman Frazier Sellers.

Contents

Chapter One

KATHERINE sped down the highway in time to her elevated heart rate. The new job pumped her up more than an extra-large latte. *Thank you, Lord, for supplying me with extra work when things are slow.*

She wheeled into the parking lot of the studio she shares with her Mom, Starling Designs, and pulled into her normal spot at the far end of the building.

She arrived a little earlier than normal and noticed her assistant's car. She knew that the building was probably still locked since Mary usually arrived very early and kept herself locked in until some of the other staff arrived. There was also a very curious vehicle filled with *men*. More unexpected customers sent by God?

The moment she stepped out of her vintage yellow Mustang, several men in military uniforms and sunglasses emerged from the vehicle and approached her.

Her steps faltered. Her gaze darted from one man to the next, each wearing a no-nonsense, serious expression. In addition, these men were after her? She took a shaky step backwards.

One gentleman lowered his sunshades, "Ms. Starling, may we have a word with you?" His serious tone jarred her to attention. She stood tall, trying not to show any fear, as the man spoke.

"What is this about?" She tried to sound confident, but her insides twisted into a jumbo-sized hot pretzel.

One of the men stretched out his hand in offer of a handshake and said, "my name is Lieutenant Jack Hancock and we are here to talk with you about a project."

Even though Katherine was a little uneasy surrounded by five men, Lieutenant Hancock's good looks did not escape her attention, and she noticed as they shook hands that he respectfully seemed to be admiring her as well. She hoped that her shoulder-length red hair was in place and that her new choice of eye shadow brought out the sparkle in her emerald green eyes. She then felt like a silly schoolgirl because she really did not know why these men were here but there was something very intriguing about Jack Hancock.

Another of the men offered, "We were sent to check out your firm before you begin work on the military base. Since the building was not yet open, we decided just to wait for someone to arrive".

"I see." She pressed her lips into a line. The woman who called from Fort Harrison Military Base must have forgotten to mention this necessity. A little forewarning would have been welcomed. She wiped sweaty hands on her pants and tried to speak without a quiver. "Come on in and I will introduce you to some of the staff, and we can discuss the matter more fully.

One of the men held the door open for the lovely but slightly jittery designer.

Mary, Katherine's long-time assistant, looked startled and dropped the documents she was working on when Katherine walked in surrounded by five relatively nice-looking men. She gave her employer a stern look. Everyone at Starling Designs knew that Mary did not like surprises, and this definitely qualified as a surprise.

"Mary, these gentlemen are from Fort Harrison Base. We will be doing some work for them, and they have a few questions for us. Do you have enough coffee made to serve them?"

Katherine's casual tone caused Mary to look even sterner, if that was possible. Mary, although petite, is definitely a no-nonsense woman with a no-nonsense salt-and-pepper bun that she had ever since Katherine could remember.

"Gentlemen, we will meet in the conference room. If you would like, I can gather more of the designers...."

"Ms. Starling, "one of the men said, "according to the nature of this assignment, we want as few people as possible to know about the work. Who is your direct supervisor?"

"My mother, Anne Starling, who is also the founder of Starling Designs, is my direct supervisor. I will see if she can meet with us." Katherine was a little annoyed that she could not tell her entire staff about the project. She did not like keeping secrets from her loyal employees.

"Since your assistant already knows about the assignment, she will need to be briefed as well."

Mary returned from the lounge with coffee and pastries for everyone, and Katherine motioned her into the conference room. "Gentlemen, if you will just wait in here, I will be back shortly with my Mother."

Katherine lightly tapped on Anne's office door and entered, then paced nervously as she waited for her mother to finish a phone call. She admired her mother who had been through so much since her husband had passed away many years before. Anne, a petite and stunning redhead with emerald green eyes never let the world see any vulnerability. Katherine knew it must have been hard to raise two children and start up a design business, but Anne had done it with competence and apparent ease.

After the call was finished, she blurted out, "Mom, this morning before I left for work, I received a call from a Leslie Midfield at Fort Harrison Base about working on some of their offices. I agreed, and when I got here, five men in an issue sedan were waiting for me. They escorted me into the building as if I was being led to walk the plank or something."

Anne motioned for her daughter to slow down. "Honey, I know about the job. Leslie Midfield called here late yesterday afternoon, and I told her she would need to check with you. Last night I had dinner with your brother and his family and forgot to mention it to you. It is okay. Leslie mentioned that some gentlemen would come over and perform an informal investigation to make sure we have no known criminals among our family skeletons."

"Mom, why didn't you tell me about this? You always do this. You tell David and even Carol everything. I am not a child. I am an adult. I work alongside you every day. Why can't you include on things like this."

"I'm sorry dear. You left early yesterday to check on a client. I was bogged down in paperwork and before I knew it, David stopped by to take me to his house. I really did just forget this time. You know I value you as a co-worker and of course, as my beautiful albeit sometimes bossy …well, sassy daughter."

Katherine's voice trembled as she asked, "Do they know about Daddy?"

"I don't know, dear, but they'll have to do the asking." Katherine noticed that her mother's grip on her ink pen tightened as she spoke. "I'm not volunteering any information. When they ask about him, I will tell them that he died in the line of duty, which to my knowledge, is what happened. You go on to the meeting, and I'll join you in just a minute."

Anne shooed her daughter out of the office. Katherine knew that her mother needed a few minutes to collect herself after the mention of David Starling, so she closed the door and left her to her thoughts.

Anne Starling gazed out the window, her eyes glazed over with tears that she refused to release this morning. There would be time for that after she went home and allowed herself to think about her husband's death, nearly forty years ago. She regained her regal poise, ran her hands through her hair, breathed a silent prayer, and headed to the conference room. As she started down the hallway, she could hear her daughter conversing with the mini-militia that had assembled in the conference room this morning.

Anne was pleased when Katherine decided to become an interior designer. She prayed for her daughter, but told her very plainly that she wanted Katherine to decide what she wanted and not to choose interior design just to please her. When Katherine graduated from the local university, she spent a summer at a Bible Camp, and by the summer's end, knew in her heart that she was called to be an interior designer. Not only did she share her mother's green eyes and red hair, they also shared a love for design.

Anne entered the room, and Katherine introduced her to their military visitors. Mary served coffee and eyed the men suspiciously, as she poured the rich, dark liquid. Anne met the men with her usual warmth, and they responded with genuine smiles.

"Mrs. Starling, we hope we haven't caused you any inconvenience," one man said, shifting as he spoke, "but we have to follow procedure."

"Relax, gentlemen – and you too, Mary and Katherine. This is just a formality. Am I right, sirs?

"Yes, we just have to make sure that everything is in the clear before you come on base. We have forms that have to be filled out, and since you will be assigned to a classified area, this must be kept 'hush-hush'. Please fill these out, and a couple of us will be back this afternoon around three to pick them up. Again, this matter is to be kept strictly confidential."

The men stood and headed to the door. Jack Hancock gave Katherine a smile and a wave as he prepared to leave the room. Katherine gave him a slight smile and hoped that she would see him again soon.

"Why did the base send five of you to deliver paperwork to a design firm?"

"Oh, we're on our way to another assignment that requires all of us. Please do not report us to that person who talks about the 'fleecing of America.' We will be busy for the rest of the day." The men actually smiled at this comment.

"Sir," Anne said, "my son David is an architect here in town, and we often consult him for assignments such as this. Would it be all right to include him in this project? Mrs. Midfield did say that some major redesigns may be needed on the upper levels of the building."

The men shifted their weight and waited for their leader to speak.

"Well...his name is David Starling. May I presume that?"

"Yes, David Starling the second," Anne returned with pride.

"May I ask if the elder David Starling will need clearance as well?" one of the men asked with just an edge of agitation.

Anne raised her shoulders just a bit. "No. My husband was killed in the line of military duty a number of years ago."

The man blushed a bit and said quietly, "I'm sorry, Mrs. Starling. I did not know. I hope I have not offended you in any way. You and your children have paid a dear price. I know. I lost my own dad a number of years ago, and he was a military man, as well. Let me just give you an extra set of forms for your son, and we'll be on our way."

Anne Starling extended her hand to the man who seemed to be in charge and thanked him for coming by. She assured them that the firm would not compromise any information about the assignment.

Upon leaving, the man leading the line of men stopped in front of an oil painting of Colonel David Starling the First. As if led by some divine hand, they each clicked their heels and saluted the painting.

The lead suit turned to Mrs. Starling and said, "Good day, ma'am. It has been our pleasure to meet you."

With that, the five of them walked in unison to the parking lot.

The ladies had followed the men to the lobby and witnessed them saluting the painting. Anne grabbed her chest, and Mary and Katherine led her to the waiting portion of the lobby and gently helped her into a leather tufted office chair. They began to ask her if it was her heart, was she okay, and did she need anything. When she did not respond to their questioning, Mary called 911.

CHAPTER TWO

"Mary, I'm going to call David," Katherine said, on the verge of tears and wanting her big brother by her side.

"Mary, it was just too much," Anne said in gasps because it was very difficult for her to breath. . "Katherine came in talking about issue sedans; then all those military men. It brought back too many memories...."

"It's okay, Annie, they cannot hurt you anymore. Only good things are in store for you and the children," Mary reassured her boss and friend, but she was more worried about her than ever before. She knew that Anne had been having some discomfort in her arms and neck but did not want her children to know. She wanted her boss, who seemed more like her own child, to be checked out by some medical folks.

Suddenly, Anne snapped to attention. "Katherine, I'm okay. You two just simmer down. Now that I have caught my breath, I am fine. You just call 911 and tell them we do not need them. Really, I'm fine."

"Uh oh," Mary said. "It's too late. I hear the sirens. You know they are just a block over."

The ambulance roared into the parking lot, and the EMTs plowed into the lobby with a stretcher. They checked Anne's heart and pulse rates, then put an oxygen mask on her and fired questions at Mary.

Anne did not like being treated as if she was not there. She kept slipping the mask off and trying to get into the conversation, but one EMT kept putting the mask back on her and trying to calm her.

About this time, David raced into the parking lot at a speed greater than that of the ambulance. He left his car door open and ran into the building so fast that an Olympic runner would have been envious. The sight of his mother in an oxygen mask did not help matters, and he began shaking.

His sister sat him down in a chair, telling him that Mother was okay and he needed to calm down for her sake.

David, being a man of God, finally remembered to breathe a word of prayer. He lowered his head, and Katherine, immediately knowing what he was doing, was ashamed that she had not prayed yet either. She lowered her head and asked for God's protection and healing power to flow over her mother.

Mary, walked by the twosome on her way to get a wet cloth for Anne, "Really", she said in her familiarly gruff manner, "I can't believe it took you two so long to think of that."

When she looked back with a smile and a wink, David and Katherine knew that Mary was as shaken as they were about their mother.

The ambulance driver stood and addressed David and Katherine and told them that he wanted to take their mother in for observation. Her heart rate and blood pressure were a little high, so just as a precaution he thought she needed to see a doctor.

Katherine grasped her brother's hand, willing his strength into her. "Are you sure that's really necessary? She keeps saying she's okay."

"It's just a precaution, but she really should be evaluated by a doctor." He removed the stethoscope from around his neck, folded it, and placed it in a black bag with his other equipment.

David squeezed her hand. "It wouldn't hurt to have her looked over. She's been ignoring this for way too long."

David and Katherine nodded. Anne told Katherine to go to her house and get a few items for her.

Mary returned with the cold compress and said, "Katherine you go on with David to the hospital and I'll come later with Annie's personal items."

Mary rang one of the secretaries on the second floor to come and cover the front desk for a few hours.

David, Katherine, and Anne all shared a glance, and he had the feeling they were all thinking the same thing he was: *What would we have done without Mary all these years?*

The EMTs wheeled Anne out into the parking lot with David, Katherine, and Mary following behind.

Anne gave Mary some last-minute instructions, and then smiled, "I know you already know all this, but I have to at least feel like I am in charge."

Mary squeezed her hand and headed back inside to give the secretary some directions before she left for Anne's house.

David motioned for Katherine to ride in the ambulance with their mother. "She needs you to hold her hand. I'll be right behind you." The two embraced, then went their separate ways.

The ride to the hospital was uneventful. Katherine prayed every inch of the way as she held her mother's hand and brushed her hair from her face, humming her mother's favorite tune, "It is well with my Soul."

While Katherine took care of the paperwork, David waited outside in the hall until they got Mrs. Starling into a hospital gown. Anne caught her breath as he came into the room. He looked very much like his father – tall with brown hair and eyes and a smile that was just a little crooked.

David tried to smile but felt more like crying. His mother holding out her hands toward him did not help matters either. They had her hooked up to several machines, but she was smiling as radiantly as ever.

"Son, everything is going to be okay. Either way things go, you know I'm going to be all right."

"I know, Mom...but we want to keep you here with us. You have to keep Katherine, the boys, and me straight and you know that Carol, your favorite daughter-in-law, is crazy about you."

Anne patted David's hand, and her eyes twinkled as she spoke. "I know, son. You are blessed with a wonderful Godly wife and two of the most energetic boys I know. Their Grandma loves them very much!"

"I know, Mom, we are all very blessed, and we want you around a long, long time. Those energetic boys, as well as Carol, Katherine, and I, all need you!" David was about to cry but kept a smile on his face for his mother.

David wanted to say more but at that moment, Anne's doctor entered the room.

Doctor Weston was well acquainted with the Starling family. He had sat by Anne's side after her husband's sudden death, helped her with the children, never charging her the full price for medical visits and treatments.

Anne did not forget the good doctor's generosity. She had more than repaid him as her business grew. She wrote references for his children as they prepared to enter college and the world of work, along with helping his wife with fundraising for the hospital, and visiting his aged mother weekly until she departed for heaven.

Doctor Weston's booming voice filled the emergency room. "What seems to be the problem, Annie?"

"How did you get assigned to me? I didn't know you covered the emergency room." Anne was happy to see her long-time friend. "I thought they would send some young whippersnapper whom I'd have to straighten out."

"I saw Mary Stennis down the hall and she filled me in. You know I can't let those whippersnappers near you. I decided to take your case myself. Annie, you rest."

Dr. Weston patted David on the shoulder and said, "How are those growing boys? It's about time for them to visit me."

As the doctor spoke, he motioned for David to step into the hall, and they headed toward the end where Katherine stood.

"I know what you two are up to," Anne called out as they moved down the hall, "and I don't like it, but I'm tired, so I'll rest for now. You'd better fill me in later though."

Katherine joined the doctor and her brother as she came down the hallway, "I just finished all that paperwork. What is going on, Dr. Weston?" Katherine said, sounding exasperated.

"Your mother is going to be fine, but I'm concerned about her heart. Do you know what brought this on? Did she just get weak or what?"

"We acquired an assignment at Fort Harrison and Dad's name came up in a meeting with some military guys. She got weak after their visit. It was kind of dramatic, but they meant no harm."

Though Katherine appreciated the way they had honored their father, she wanted to punch them for the effect it had on her mother.

"What assignment, Sis?" David asked.

"A design project over at the base. Mom made sure that you will be cleared." Katherine lowered her voice. "Doctor Weston, I just remembered, I wasn't supposed to say anything about it. You know, top-secret military stuff. Please do not say anything. I don't know if we will do the job or not." Katherine felt like biting her tongue off. She hoped her loose lips would not cost the design firm this new job.

"Oh, I feel sure your mother will still want the job. This could be an answer to prayer. It might take her mind off anything that may be causing stress…but she needs her rest. I am going to admit her and move her into a room until tomorrow. Then she needs complete bed rest at home for a while." Doctor Weston was making notes while he was talking. "If I know Annie, she won't rest until she gets back to work, so let her do light paperwork, but you two handle the brunt of the military project."

David looked very inquisitively at him. "Doctor, why do you say this may be an answer to prayer?"

"I'll let Annie tell you that when she's ready. She would have my head on a platter if I gave away too much information – and don't you start in with too many questions this afternoon. There'll be plenty of time for that later."

CHAPTER THREE

THE doctor completed his notes, and then headed toward the front of the hospital. "Oh, I am going to order a heart catheterization to check her arteries, just to be on the safe side."

"Remember, she has to rest." As he turned the corner, he saw Mary Stennis. He looked back at David and Katherine and said with a smile, "If anyone can make Annie Starling rest, it's Mary. I'm going to put her on alert." The doctor looked back again. "Oh, and your secret is safe with me."

At that, he waved and headed toward Mary.

After Mary received instructions from Dr. Weston, she walked toward David and Katherine. Katherine gave her a hug, "I know you hate hospitals after all the time you spent in them when Uncle Webb went through chemo and radiation. Tears began to sting Mary's eyes as she thought of her beloved husband, Webb. Oh, how she still misses him!

Anne and her family were all the family she had now, and they had no idea how important they were to her. If there was anything the Starling family needed, Mary would do her best to get it. Now that Annie needed attention, Mary would see that she got it, even if it meant that she herself got no rest.

Mary approached David and Katherine at first showing very little emotion, and then she softened and grabbed them around the shoulders. "We're going to get through this," she said. "The Lord is going to see us through this, and your Mother is going to be okay. I feel a peace about this. She needs rest and some medication, but she is going to be with us for a while. I don't think I could handle losing her too."

Mary loved David and Katherine as if they were her own children. They had referred to her and Webb as, Uncle Webb and Aunt Mary, when they were little. However, after Webb's passing, Mary had insisted that the children (who were then grown) call her Mary, instead of Aunt Mary. She felt like it was more professional for their businesses, and she was a stickler for protocol.

David, Katherine, and Mary walked back to see Anne, who slept peacefully, so they talked with the nurse.

"We have her room ready and are taking her up now, but she needs to sleep for at least a couple of hours."

Once again, Mary snapped to attention, "Katherine, you go and fill out the paperwork for the base. David, you go and check on your firm and Carol and the boys. I am staying here. I brought toiletries and a gown for Annie. Go on, you two, and check back in a couple of hours."

David and Katherine knew that there was no point in arguing with the little dynamo. They each kissed their mother's brow softly, hugged Mary, and then headed out to David's car.

As they drove back to the design firm, he questioned his sister. "Tell me about this assignment for the military."

Katherine informed him of the day's events and brought him up to speed on their new project. "Mother wants the job. She told them that she has a son who is an architect, and they granted you clearance. Mary also has clearance."

"I offered to call in some of our other designers," she went on, "but the men wanted to keep it to as few people as possible. The meeting had some dramatics. Mother told them that her son's name is David Starling the Second and one of the men asked – a little tersely, I might add – if David the First would need clearance. Mom told them quite courageously that he lost his life in the line of military duty. Well, he was embarrassed by his mistake. He mentioned that his dad was a military man and had lost his life as well. On the way out, they noticed the oil painting of Dad and saluted it. I know they meant well, but it was right after that when Mom collapsed."

"This may have quickened the inevitable, but I have been worried about Mom for some time," David said in a hushed tone.

"I know. We have both tried to tell her to slow down, but you know Mom. She just won't stop." Katherine silently prayed that her mother would heed the doctor's and Mary's orders, and get some rest.

Chapter Four

WHEN they arrived at the design-firm parking lot, a brown sedan had just driven up. The handsome man from this morning emerged from the vehicle. He was alone this time.

"Well, here's Mister Military," Katherine said. "I guess he wants the forms, but they haven't been touched yet."

David tried unsuccessfully to hide his grin. "Maybe this is my new brother-in-law."

"Oh, you go on and tend to your business and family. I do not think we will be seeing this guy after today." Katherine smiled as she waved her brother on his way.

"Ms. Starling. I do not think I ever introduced myself this morning. I am Lieutenant Jack Hancock. I was in the area and decided to drop by to see if you've completed the forms."

"Mister...I mean Lieutenant."

"Just call me, Jack."

"Okay, but only if you call me Katherine. Jack, we had a bit of a scare, and I am afraid we have not touched the forms. I'm sure I can have them for you later today."

"What happened?" He sounded genuinely concerned. "Anything I can help you with?"

"No, not really. My mom had an attack of some sort, and they are checking her now. She wants to continue with the assignment, but she will be working from her bedroom. My brother, Mrs. Stennis, and I will do the...."

"Oh, was that your brother?" Jack sounded more relieved that he intended to. He hoped Katherine did not notice his relief.

"Yes, that was David. He will make any major re-design decisions for us. Come in, and we'll have a look at those forms over tea or lemonade."

Katherine was beginning to realize that she liked being around this guy. He seemed very nice and she enjoyed talking with him. She liked his blonde hair and green eyes but especially his boyish grin. Yes, she could get used to being around Jack Hancock.

"How is your mom?" he asked as he held the door open for Katherine. "I hope it's nothing serious."

"She is resting right now but they have her under observation. We feel like she will be okay, but Mom has been under a lot of stress, and we want to be sure she is fine before she comes home.

Katherine stopped at Michelle Baldwin's desk and checked her phone messages. "Michelle, please send out an email that there will be a staff meeting at four o'clock in the conference room. I want to inform everyone of mother's condition, and then I'll be leaving to go back to the hospital."

"Yes, ma'am. I'll type that up right now." Michelle turned immediately to the computer.

"Let's meet in the conference room. I just have to find those forms." Katherine started looking through files on Mary's desk.

"Ms. Starling, I think these are the forms you are looking for." Michelle handed Katherine a manila envelope. "Before Mrs. Stennis left, she gave me instructions on how to fill them out, and I have them here. I hope I completed them correctly."

"Why, thank you Michelle. Yes, yes, I am sure these are fine. I will just go over them with Jack, I mean Lieutenant Hancock. Thank you. This will save me an hour or so. In fact, change that meeting to three o'clock instead of four, and I'll get back to the hospital earlier."

Katherine seated herself across the big mahogany table from Jack Hancock. "Mary left instructions with Michelle to fill out the forms, and she did. I will glance over them, and then you can do the same. Would you like some tea or lemonade? I didn't mean to forget my hospitality, but it has been a long day."

"No, no. I'm fine."

Jack was anything but fine. Butterflies flapped against his stomach like bats as he gazed at the lovely Katherine Starling, but he did his best to keep his cool. He cleared his throat and tried to sound unaffected.

"Well, everything seems to be in order," he said finally. "If you have any questions before then, please give us a call." He gave her his business card and hoped he would hear from her very soon.

Katherine took his business card and placed it on the table. She then extended her hand to the lieutenant. She longed to talk with him and find out everything about him, but she had a meeting to get to and then back to the hospital.

"Thank you, Katherine, and I hope your mother recovers soon. Maybe we will run into each other on base."

He let himself out and headed toward the parking lot. As he drove back toward base, he prayed.

"Father, thank you for letting me meet that beautiful creature, Katherine Starling. What a breath of fresh air. Please touch her mother, Mrs. Starling. If Katherine is someone, you want in my life, tender her heart and give me favor in her eyes. Give me wisdom as I pursue her, and unless You give me orders otherwise, that is what I intend to do.

"I saw the Christian plaques and symbols all over the design firm, and I believe she is Your daughter. This is what I have been asking for, Lord, a woman who loves you with all of her heart, and maybe she is the one. Thank you, Lord, for working this situation out in the way You intend for it to work. In Jesus' name. Amen."

Katherine had a few minutes before the staff meeting. She went into her office and sat at her desk for a few moments, numb from the day's events. She was also anxious to get back to the hospital. She slumped in her chair for a few moments and then sat up, realizing all that she had to do.

In spite of herself, she was a little more than starry-eyed over Lieutenant Hancock. She felt as if he was a believer, because he was wearing a little fish tie tack. She also knew that she had not felt about a man this way in a long time. Her pulse quickened when he was near and she could still remember the smell of his cologne.

Katherine pushed Jack from her mind and picked up some files to review.

I have entirely too much going on in my life to become involved with a man, right now!

David went to his office and checked with his secretary for phone messages and appointments. Then he hurried to a phone to call Carol. In the hullabaloo, he had forgotten to call her, and he needed to talk to her.

"Hello."

The sound of her voice made David forget his troubles for a moment.

"Carol, honey, I'm sorry I didn't call you earlier, but Mom's in the hospital."

"What's wrong? Which hospital? What happened?"

David could tell by Carol's voice that she was upset. She loved her mother-in-law very much. In fact, Carol's mother died several years earlier, and since then she had leaned on Anne for maternal support.

"Not so fast. She is going to be okay, we think. She collapsed this morning at the firm. She is at Central Memorial under Doctor Weston's care. She has to have lots of rest, but I really think she will be fine. I'm going to wrap things up here and head back over, so I may run a little late for dinner."

David was really trying to convince himself that everything would be fine with his mother. He knew if anyone could reassure him it would be Carol.

At two fifty-five, Michelle Baldwin knocked on Katherine's office door and reminded her of the meeting.

Katherine thanked Michelle for her reminder.

"Can I tell the staff that you will be in the conference room soon?"

"Yes, I'll be there in a few minutes." Katherine checked her image in the mirror hanging by her door, fluffed her hair a little, and headed to the meeting.

Chapter Five

KATHERINE entered the conference room, where most of the staff had assembled. She addressed the other five designers, the firm's accountant, and the remaining secretary. The meeting lasted about fifteen minutes as she filled them in on her mother's condition, explaining that they should wait until the doctor's okay to pay her a visit, but e-mails and text messages would be welcome.

They went over existing accounts and pending projects, excluding the military assignment. Katherine wished that she could include the staff, because they had some of the most gifted designers in the country, and they would love the opportunity to offer suggestions for a project that would be a bit more stark and traditional than many of their jobs.

Peggy McCoy, an active member of Anne's Sunday School class, asked if anyone minded if she prayed for Mrs. Starling's speedy recovery. She looked intently at Morgan Rieman, an outspoken atheist who knew that the statement was meant for him. Morgan loved the Starlings and suspected that they, along with Mary Stennis and Peggy, were praying for him and his family.

He nodded at Peggy and said in his Southern drawl, "I think that would be a good idea in this situation."

Everyone at Glenview First Baptist knew that Peggy McCoy shook the rafters of Heaven when she prayed, and this time was no different. Katherine was grateful for friends and relatives who trusted in the power of God, and she was also glad that Morgan was present. She made a note in her mind to relay this to her mother. She knew that when she heard this, Anne would be on the phone to her church's prayer chain to step up the prayers for Morgan and his family.

Katherine thanked Peggy for her prayer and, after hugs all around, left the building with a renewed confidence that God was in fact all-powerful. Just as she left the parking lot, her cell phone rang.

"Hello, this is Katherine Starling."

"Katherine, this is Mary. Everything is okay, but I wonder if you would mind swinging by my place and picking up a few things for me."

"Mary, I insist on staying tonight." Katherine knew that if Mary had made up her mind, her words were a waste of time.

"Katherine Starling, did you understand what I said? I said I would stay with your mother tonight. She will need a lot of care for quite some time, so let me take care of her tonight, and you can go over to her place later and get things ready there." Mary's tone of voice was insistent.

Mary finished the conversation with her litany of items that she needed from her place, promptly ending with no further discussion of who would spend the night with Anne.

Katherine knew there was no use arguing with Mary Stennis about this. She turned her car toward her dear friend's place in order to gather up the commanded items. Once she had followed Mary's orders, she headed toward the hospital, pulling into the parking lot just before sunset. She allowed herself to sit still just a moment and gaze at the beautiful display of the various shades and tints of colors that painted the sky. She breathed a prayer of thanks for God's goodness and mercy and then headed to check on her Mom and Mary.

Katherine entered her mother's room and gave Mary her overnight items.

Mary thanked Katherine and motioned her out into the hallway. "Your mom has slept peacefully all afternoon, but Doctor Weston wants to do a few more tests tomorrow just for precautionary measures. He wants to keep her until day after tomorrow. He said Anne complained of tiredness a few weeks ago, and he told her to come in for the tests then, but she put it off. Now he has her where he wants her and is not letting her go until he finds out what's going on."

Katherine was genuinely concerned for her mother, but she was relieved that Doctor Weston seemed to have a handle on the situation. She and Mary embraced shortly, then re-entered her mother's room.

Anne stirred in the bed, and opened her eyes. After blinking several times to wake up, she said, "I'm hungry". Katherine alerted the nurses' station, and they brought a tray filled with a delicious culinary fare of clear chicken broth and strawberry gelatin. Anne winched when she saw the tray and the nurse who brought it, pointed to a little card that said, 'liquid diet'. 'We are pushing it a little with the gelatin', the young nurse stated the obvious.

Anne nodded and said, 'I know, no 'real' solid food until after the tests'. She did eat all of the broth and gelatin because she knew that would be it for a while.

David and Carol dropped by but did not stay long, and Katherine, realizing that Mary meant business about staying the night, accompanied them to the parking lot. They shared concerns about their mother, and then headed to their respective homes.

That night Anne had a series of nightmares.

It was Easter Sunday, April 22, 1962, and she sat in the sheriff's office in Graham County, Florida, with her in-laws.

The sheriff stated simply, "Mrs. Starling, your husband is dead. The boarding-house owner found him early this morning with a bullet wound in his head. Apparent suicide. You will need to go to the town where he was working and talk with the authorities there. I am sorry, but that is all the information I have. If you need me, you can reach me here at my office."

Anne knew the last thing in the world that she wanted was to contact that horrid little man who had dropped the news of her husband's death like a bomb.

Bombs, bombs, bombs – she could see the blasts and almost feel the heat. She could hear her husband calling her name, calling their children's names. She was running to him. Then a big atomic blast came between them, and when the smoked cleared, he was gone.

She awoke, bolted up in bed, as she called her husband's name.

Mary, who had comforted Anne so many times, went to her bedside and held her. She prayed silently, then aloud, then silently again until Anne drifted off to sleep. She then settled back in her place on the hospital's excuse for a cot, but her mind did not settle.

She thought back to the first time she comforted her dear friend, when David and Katherine were quite young, and both had very bad colds. Anne was exhausted from working all-day and staying up with them at night. Finally, with Webb's blessing, Mary told Anne that she would be staying day and night until the children were better.

The second night Anne woke up screaming and jabbering about bombs and rockets. Mary brought her warm milk and stayed with her until she went back to sleep. In the next few days, Anne told Mary and Webb her suspicions about her husband's death.

Anne, Mary, and Webb before he passed, had all been praying for years for the story to be uncovered. *Maybe this military assignment will help,* Mary thought.

Anne had not yet felt it the right time to burden David and Katherine, but she admitted to Mary just a few weeks earlier, that she felt they needed to be told soon.

One of the night nurses coming in to check Anne's vitals and drip interrupted Mary's thoughts. Fortunately, Anne kept right on sleeping peacefully until two nurses came in the next morning to get her ready for the tests that Dr. Weston had ordered.

Early the next morning, Katherine called her mother's room, and Mary answered.

"Dear, they have taken her down for tests. She should be back in the room at about ten o'clock. I think she is going to be fine.

"I'm going to swing by there on the way to work and let you go home, because you're going to want to come back later."

"You do have that meeting at noon, but come by this morning. Peggy is going to relieve you at eleven o'clock to give you time to get to the base. I will come back later this afternoon. I do know my limits. I'll get some rest before I return." Mary continued the conversation by reminding Katherine of her schedule for the day, just as she had done so many times at the firm. Katherine knew very well that Mary was quite an asset to the firm. She kept everyone on schedule.

"Mary, let me stay tonight or at least relieve you about nine o'clock," she almost pleaded, feeling somewhat helpless.

Mary sensed Katherine's feelings and finally relented. "All right, you can come at nine, but I'll be back early in the morning to relieve you."

"Good. I will be there in a few minutes. Are you still drinking your coffee black?"

"Yes, no pollutants for me and hot, hot." Mary was pleased that Katherine remembered. The hospital staff was very generous, but their coffee was just not strong enough for this lady.

As Katherine ran out the door with thermos in hand, David pulled into her driveway.

"Hop in," he said, "and I'll take you to the hospital so we can talk for a few minutes. I know you'll need your car later, so I'll bring you back after we visit awhile."

"Well, I'm staying until eleven, so Mary can go home and get some rest. That is okay. I will stay a while, and then Carol will come and bring you back here. Come on. I have some of Carol's cinnamon rolls – her great-grandmother's recipe." David enticed Katherine to try his wife's breakfast treat.

"Okay." Katherine hated herself for succumbing to Carol's cinnamon rolls, but they were her favorite and her mother's favorite too. The sugary scent of Carol's famous cinnamon rolls won out, she did take one off the plate to enjoy during their ride to the hospital.

"Sis, I'm really worried about Mom. Doctor Weston called last night and said he scheduled more tests this morning. Do you know exactly what's going on?"

"Mary just said that Doctor Weston is going to conduct all the tests that he can while he has Mom corralled. I don't know what exactly is going on, but she's in good hands, and you know the prayer chain at church hasn't stopped since we called them yesterday." Katherine tried to sound more confident than she felt, but she knew she was not fooling her brother for a minute.

"Katherine, there's another reason I wanted to talk with you. Doctor Weston also said that there are things about our father's death that we do not know, and he is worried that Mom is going to become overwhelmed and stressed with this military project. At first he thought it would be a good idea, but he doesn't want her unnecessarily excited."

"What things don't we know?" Katherine's green eyes widened as she questioned her brother. Katherine could not believe that her mom had withheld information from them.

"He didn't say. He wants to let Mom tell us, but he does not want us to prod and poke for information until she is up to it – which according to him could be a while. Let's leave it up to her to decide that, but if she wants to keep the military project, we do all the work."

"You know Mom will have to involve herself in some way. How are we going to handle that?"

Approaching the hospital parking lot, David looked at his younger sister and said, "Well, that leaves one thing. Let's pray."

David and Katherine entered the room to find Anne eating a sparse breakfast of different juices and other unidentified liquids.

When Mary caught a whiff of Carol's cinnamon rolls, she shooed them out of the room. "Doctor Weston said she shouldn't eat rich foods right now."

"It's all right, Mary," Anne called. "All of you come back in here this instant. David, thank Carol for the cinnamon rolls, and Mary, will you wrap some up for me to have later today? Now come on around and tell me all the news." Anne winked at them, and they all sighed, relieved.

"The boys made you this card," David told her, fidgeting nervously with his watchband, "and Carol is coming later this morning."

His mother leaned toward him and put a reassuring finger on the watch. "Son, I feel fine this morning. Doctor Weston is going to fix me up real soon."

As always, David felt better after hearing his mother's reassuring voice. However, this time he was worried for her. He knew that she would put on a happy face, even if she was still not feeling well.

Carol arrived later in the morning armed with flowers and new pictures of the grandsons, the apples of their Grandma Annie's eye.

When the nurses came and took Anne for a last round of tests, Katherine and Carol sat and talked for a few minutes. Carol looked with concern at her sister-in-law who slumped in her chair. "How are you holding up, Sis?"

"I am okay, a bit worried but okay. Mom will be fine. I just know this has taken a toll on her and she has got to start resting more."

"Good luck with that." Carol slightly chuckled as she spoke. She could not imagine her energetic mother-in-law slowing down one bit.

"I know but we have got to find a way to get her to slow down." Katherine sighed as she considered what a task that would be for all concerned.

Chapter Six

Peggy McCoy arrived right on time with her Bible, a Sunday School lesson book, magazines, and crossword puzzles, a favorite pastime of Anne's.

"Anne may not feel like doing any of this, but just in case, I brought it anyway. I'll leave the magazines so if anyone else needs something to read, they'll be here."

Peggy was one of Anne's favorite people. Anne often remarked how she enjoyed going to church and working with her. Katherine was thankful that she would be spending time with her mother.

Carol dropped off her sister-in-law at her house and said, "Katherine, you are a gorgeous lady, but I'll give you the same advice that my stylish Great Aunt Ruby would give me about dating. Re-apply that lip color, pinch your cheeks, and bend over, then throw you hair back to give it some fluff. The base is going to be crawling with men."

"I am just having lunch with Leslie Midfield. Okay, okay, I'll take your advice, but I don't know what the big deal is."

Carol waved and grinned as she backed out of the driveway. Katherine knew that Carol had detected the excitement in her voice when she had told her about Jack Hancock in an earlier conversation.

She checked her watch and snapped to attention, then unlocked the door and ran to her bedroom to inspect herself in front of the big mirror.

Not bad, she thought. *Not bad....*

She headed to the bathroom, where she re-applied lip and cheek color but decided against pinching herself. She bent over and ran the dryer through her hair. When she stood up, she looked like a character from

Spook Alley. She quickly got her comb, worked on her hair, then swung by the big mirror for a final inspection and headed out the door, toward her destiny.

Katherine followed Leslie's directions to the dining hall. Her low-heeled pumps click clacked on the linoleum as she passed door after door. After two more turns, the commissary door sat at the end of the hallway. She checked her watch; five minutes to spare. Good, she had time to call the hospital.

"Hello, Anne Starling's room".

"Peggy, how is she doing?"

"Oh, she is resting. The nurses have kept a check on her but she seems fine at the moment."

"Peggy, thank you so much for staying with Mom. I will be in later this evening but if you need to go, the nurses will keep a watch on her."

"I am in no hurry. Just take your time and whoever gets here first can relieve me."

She spotted Leslie already seated at a table, motioning for Katherine to join her. Katherine was pleased to see her smiling face and felt immediately at ease.

"I hope you don't mind," Leslie said, "but I went ahead and ordered iced tea and told them we'd have the buffet."

"Oh, that's fine. It will save me the trouble of ordering."

"Jack told me that your mother is in the hospital. I am so sorry to hear that. How is she doing?"

Katherine told Leslie that her mother was progressing along and that every precaution was being taken to ensure her health.

"Jack Hancock!" Leslie exclaimed. "How are you today? Please join us for lunch. I believe you have met Katherine Starling. "

Jack hoped that Katherine could not see his heart pounding underneath his uniform. "Yes, yes," he said. "I met Katherine yesterday. How is your mother doing today?"

"Well, she's doing okay. Tests are being run, but we hope to have her home soon. You look just as polished today as you did yesterday." Katherine gestured to indicate that she was referring to his uniform.

"Oh, right. I was at an officers' meeting earlier. Leslie, if it's okay with Katherine I think I'll join you."

Katherine nodded, and Jack seated himself at the table with the two ladies. Afterwards, Leslie began to explain the project to Katherine." Miss Starling, as I told you, we have received funds to redecorate the old administration building. Some of the offices have been closed since the Cold War. You know, there were many hush-hush activities back then, and many offices were completely sealed off. Well, I do not know if you have noticed, but atomic-bomb test films are being declassified right and left now, and it is kind of silly to be so secretive about something that took place so long ago.

"Some of the officers feel that we need more space and that we may as well make use of what's already here rather than using the taxpayers' money to construct more buildings."

Leslie took a breath, hoping that she had not disclosed anything that is top secret but she also thought that Katherine probably would not notice anyway.

I think this project will be challenging. It's as if we get a little look at history that's been frozen in space, then thaw that frozen space to make it useful to our government and ultimately to us the 'taxpayers.' As far as I'm concerned, it will be an honor to take the job." Katherine really meant this. She was also glad for the chance to work near Jack Hancock.

"I should think it *would* be quite challenging," Jack chimed, "to see government 'frozen in space,' as you so aptly put it, then make it available to this generation."

Leslie looked at her watch and announced, "I have an appointment in just a few minutes. Katherine, is there a time when you and your brother can meet me at the old administration building in the next few days? Maybe you need to see to your mother first, and then get back with me."

"Why don't I call you tomorrow when I know more about Mom's condition and how often my brother and I will be needed at home?"

With that, Leslie went to the cashier, signed a ticket, and headed out of the dining hall. This left Katherine and Jack alone at the little table. They made light conversation briefly, and then he decided to go for broke. "Katherine, I certainly have enjoyed our meal together, even if I crashed the party."

"Oh, I'm glad you did. I enjoyed our time together." Katherine felt so starry-eyed; she hoped she was not flapping her eyelashes to match the butterflies in her stomach.

"I know you're uncertain about your mother's condition, but would you mind if I called you in a day or two to check on her? Then if you are free, maybe we could go to a movie, dinner, whatever you would like to do." Jack fidgeted nervously as he waited for her answer.

"Please do give me a call."

It was then Katherine's turn to find her business card in her purse. She handed it to the dashing young 'military man'. "This has my business and cell-phone numbers. I look forward to hearing from you."

"I will call – and please let me take care of the ticket for lunch if Leslie didn't."

An officer who outranked him called Jack to another table. He wanted to walk Katherine to her car, but "duty called."

Katherine almost floated to her car. She could not believe it. It had been quite some time since she met someone as nice, good-looking, and professional as Mr. err... Lt. Colonel Hancock. She was almost sure of his faith, because before the meal he asked permission to say grace. From his choice of words and tone, she knew he was speaking to Someone he knew personally.

Katherine's cell phone rang as she started her car.

"Hello."

"Katherine, this is Michelle at the office. I was wondering if you could come by here on your way home."

"Yes. Is there a problem?"

"Oh, no, but I need your signature on some documents. I can't find the stamp pad, and I really don't think I'm authorized to use the signature pad." Michelle sounded a bit overwhelmed.

"Okay, I'll be there in about thirty minutes. I was coming by there anyway to check messages, assignments, and mother's mail. I'm on the way."

Katherine clicked the cell phone off and went back to dreaming about Jack Hancock.

CHAPTER SEVEN

"SHE's on her way!" Michelle ran about the room to get everyone into position and ready for Katherine's arrival.

"Make sure that everything is ready. I'll bet she hasn't even remembered that today is her birthday."

The men made sure that enough chairs were in place and the ladies put cups, plates, forks, and napkins on the conference table. The cake for Katherine's birthday was decorated to look like several swatches of fabric with the message: *If none of these please you, we can look at some others*", a phrase that she said many times each day.

Michelle herded everyone into the conference room and shut the door. Just in time before Katherine drove into the parking lot. Michelle scurried to her normal position.

Katherine strode through the door with a perplexed expression on her face. "Why is David's car here? Is something wrong with Mom?"

"He's in the conference room along with some papers that need your signature."

Katherine opened the door to the conference room.

Everyone gathered in the room shouted, "Surprise!"

Katherine's twin nephews, David Ill (Trey) and Trevor, raced toward her and gave their Auntie Katherine a big birthday hug.

A startled Katherine said, "I have a sneaking feeling that Mom is at the bottom of this. Am I right?"

"Yes, you are, Ms. Starling. She had Mary call from the hospital today, and I picked up the cake that she ordered days ago. The paper goods were hidden in the break room, and we rummaged for candles."

Katherine actually made two wishes – that her mother would be okay and that Jack Hancock would call her this weekend.

She blew out all the candles, thinking, *who knows what may happen in the next few days.*

After a few minutes of food and fellowship, everyone went back to work. David told Katherine that they were headed to the hospital.

"I'm going to relieve Mary at nine o'clock," she responded. "I'll probably get there about eight or a little after and see if I can manage to get her to agree to go home. I thought this place would fall apart without her around, but Michelle has kept it in shipshape."

"Well, don't let Mary hear you say that," David said. "Now I can spend the night if you need me."

"So can I, Katherine," Carol told her. "You and Mary don't forget us. We want to help."

"I know, but you save your energy for next week when Mom starts popping out orders for everyone." Katherine was thankful to have such a loving brother and sister-in-law.

"Tell Mom that I'm checking our messages and mail and will be there soon." Katherine grinned as she added, "I also have some 'military romance' news to tell her."

"Oh, tell us," Carol almost squealed. "We've been dying to hear."

"Well, one Lieutenant Jack Hancock just happened to be in the dining hall while I was lunching with Leslie Midfield, and he joined us. Leslie left first, and we had an opportunity to talk. When Mom gets better, he wants to get together with me." Katherine's eyes danced as she talked about her new romantic interest.

"So, can I assume I am finally getting a brother-in-law?" David looked like the cat that caught the canary.

"Not so fast, Big Brother. Let's let 'Military Guy' cool his heels for a while." She knew that her grin was giving away her real feelings.

"That's right, Katherine. That's what I did with your brother here." Carol looked smugly at her husband. "We'll just pray him in like we did this one. Then he came running."

"It's the best deal I ever got," David gave his wife a loving poke, "and if Mister...I mean, Lieutenant Hancock is a Christian and has any brains, he'll come running to Red here. In fact, ladies, I'll help you 'pray him in,' or maybe you meant to say *reel* him in."

"If I could have just a little bit of what you two have and if he and I are a good match," Katherine told him, "then yes, let's pray him in. Then maybe I can reel him in, or maybe we should pray that the Lord will reel him in for us. We will figure it out as we go along. Tell Mom I'll be there soon — but don't tell her the rest." Katherine looked with admiration at her brother and sister-in-law and felt happiness well up inside of her that she might be on the brink of having a similar relationship in her own life.

Katherine kissed her nephews. Then the four were off to see Grandma Annie.

"So," Katherine drew out the word, "where are those papers that needed my signature?" she asked in a teasing way.

"We didn't know if you would come in or if you might wait until later after we were all gone. We just had to get you in here."

"I understand, and I'm glad you did. I do wish Mom could have been here. By the way, thanks for saving Mary and Peggy some cake. It was nice to be remembered and even nicer to know Mom cared enough to pull it off from her hospital bed. That is my mom — the original atomic dynamo. I...."

Suddenly Katherine was reminded of her conversation with Leslie Midfield. If memory served her correctly, the Cold War was about atomic bombs, tests, and such — and she thought her dad might have been involved in some of the tests. She could not remember an exact conversation but she thought she had overheard her Mom talking with Mary about it.

Oh, well, I will have to ask Mom or David about it later.

At her computer, Katherine composed a message to update all of those expressing concern about her mother, but her mind wandered back to her conversation with Leslie.

Atomic testing, what did it all mean?

CHAPTER EIGHT

KATHERINE's mind was so tired that thinking felt like an Olympic sport she could not qualify for at this moment. She did try to think of Jack Hancock but those thoughts were interrupted by her office phone.

"Yes?"

"Ms. Starling, Mary Stennis is on line one."

"Thank you, Michelle." She picked up the phone. "Hello, Mary. Is anything wrong?"

"Oh, no. Quite the contrary. Anne has taken a turn for the better."

"For the better?"

"Yes. Her pulse and heart rates have evened out, and Doctor Weston and his staff cannot find anything wrong with her. As a precaution he doesn't want her released until in the morning, and he still wants her to take it easy for a few days."

"Praise the Lord. Our prayers have been answered. Of course, we'll have our hands full trying to keep that little keg of dynamite down."

"Yes, I know, but I think she'll honor the doctor's wishes to a degree anyway. She gave us a scare, but I think she got one as well."

"Mary, thank you so much for helping us with Mom. I'll be in around eight-thirty to relieve you, I know you are exhausted." Katherine breathed a prayer of thanks as she waited for Mary's response.

"You know I think of Annie as my own daughter. I would not have it any other way but to help out. I will let you relieve me though. Since I know she's going to be okay, I'll go on home and rest, 'cause she'll need me later." Mary was thankful for Anne's recovery but also a little afraid to become too excited. After losing Webb, she could not bear it if anything happened to Anne.

They said their goodbyes and Katherine breathed a prayer for her dear friend. *Lord, thank you for Mary; please bless her in a very special way.*

She busied herself with the loose ends in her office, and then went to her mother's office to clear out some of her e-mail messages along with the mail that was accumulating on her desk. Most of the messages were friendly greetings from associates and friends who didn't' know that Ann was in the hospital – but one subject line caught Katherine's attention. The message was from a space center in another state, and the subject was *Cold War Info.*

Katherine curiously clicked into the message, not knowing what to expect. It was a simple message:

> *Mrs. Starling, I have some information concerning your late husband's death. I have listed a couple of websites that might be of value to you. As an employee of the space center, I can tell you little, but I do wish you the best in your search for answers.*

The message was not signed, but at the bottom was a series of letters and numbers: *IS4031.*

Katherine looked intently at the message and at the code. She then thought of her mother's favorite verse: Isaiah 40:31. *Could this be what the sender meant? Probably not, but that is a good verse.*

She mentally went over the verse in her mind: *"But they that wait upon the Lord shall renew their strength; they shall mount up with wings as eagles; they shall run, and not be weary; and they shall walk, and not faint."*

Her Mom had told her that her dad died during some testing procedures, and she just accepted that something had malfunctioned, causing his death. Apparently, her mom believed there was more to the story and was trying to get to the bottom of it. Katherine stared into the distance for a bit, drumming her fingers on the desk as she mulled this over in her mind.

Upon finishing her work, Katherine locked up the office for the night and headed to her car. Isaiah 40:31 kept going repeatedly in her mind. *A lovely verse...but is the Lord saying something about Dad's death through it?*

Katherine breathed a prayer asking God for guidance. David would be very interested in this, too, but…. It was getting late, so she headed to the hospital. She would keep it to herself for now.

She arrived to find her mom laughing and talking with David and his family. The boys ran and hugged her as they did each time they saw their Aunt Katherine. They chatted for a few minutes, and then David asked if they could all pray together before they headed home.

Father, thank you so much for restoring Mom's health. We ask you to bless her with continued health and strength. Help the rest of us to know how to meet her needs, and please encourage her to 'take things easy for awhile'. We love you Father and once again, thank you for watching over all of us and especially Mom who is usually the one taking care of everyone else. Help her to slow down and let us return the favor. We pray these things in Your Son's precious name, Amen.

After the prayer David, Carol, and the boys said their good-byes, leaving Katherine and her mother alone in the room.

Anne sensed that something bothered her daughter, "Katherine, what's wrong, dear? The doctor said that I'm better, so why the long face?"

"What are you talking about? Of course, I am glad you are doing better. I'm just worried you won't take it easy like the doctor said." Katherine tried to hide her puzzlement about the e-mail message, even though she knew her mother could always "read her like a book." It was no use trying to hide the news any longer; she could not avoid the 'mother look' that Anne gave her. She finally broke down and told her mom about the message and the verse at the end.

"I see." Anne took a deep breath. "I've been meaning to tell you and David about my suspicions concerning your father's death, and I guess now is as good a time as any.

"Your dad was a fine man, and you know I was devastated when he died. We were told that some of his designs for the launch vehicles had caused major problems with the test and that David committed suicide after the test because he could not handle the pressure. Well, at the time I was heartbroken and had you and David to take care of, so I did not question it.

"As time went on, I began to receive little messages in the mail, just short notes that said things like, *David Starling was murdered, and so were others.* None of them had an address or name on the notes, and they all had different postmarks."

"Because Mary and Webb helped us out so much, I confided in them, and they were afraid for me. One day Mary had you and David at the park, and I went home to start supper and found that the apartment had been broken into. All the police could find missing were the notes that I had received about your Father. We stayed with Webb and Mary that night, and they insisted that we not return to that apartment.

"We stayed with them until we found another apartment closer to them, and that put us on the other end of town. Webb said if anything strange happened again, all of us- including the two of them- would move to another town. Nothing else happened. Webb, Mary, and I prayed for revelation, but no more messages came.

"Then several years ago I was watching a talk show, and a lady whose husband died the same year as your dad was being interviewed. She was telling about his life and his magnificent work with the space program. He mysteriously disappeared and had not been heard from since. I tried to contact her through the network, but they would not give her real name or address. I know there are people who know something but none are talking. Something devastating happened, and whatever it was, cost many people their lives."

"Oh, Mom, do you think we will ever find out the truth?" Katherine was shocked by the information and knew that except by the grace of God they would not get to the bottom of it.

"By God's good grace we *will* know the truth, and the truth will set us free," Anne Starling said, having settled in her mind years ago that by God's divine revelation they would know exactly what happened to not only her husband but also the many other men who died that weekend or who were never heard from again.

Chapter Nine

Anne had a restful night, and Katherine helped her put on her most luxurious robe and slippers. Anne had a love for style not only in interior design, but also in fashion.

After Dr. Weston released Anne from the hospital, Katherine vowed to keep the conversation light on the drive home.

"Kat, the first thing that I want you to do when we get home is print out that e-mail message and let me take a look at it."

"Don't you think you should rest this afternoon and look at it tomorrow?" Katherine knew that her mother's mind was made up, but she attempted to dissuade her anyway.

"Do you think I'm going to rest until I see that message?" Anne's spirits were skyrocketing. She felt the hand of God in the situation, and she wanted to tackle it as soon as possible.

"I guess not, but do let me fix you some soup and a sandwich before we get started."

"I'll give you thirty minutes to get what you want to get done, and then I want that printout."

Anne chuckled to herself. Katherine loved working with a deadline, so she had given her one. She could hardly wait to get her hands on the e-mail.

They arrived at the house, where the grandsons had left Grandma a welcome-home banner that they made. The boys had their grandma wrapped around their pinky fingers, and they knew it.

Katherine helped Anne to her bedroom, and then went in her mom's gourmet kitchen. She then prepared a simple fare of tomato soup and a grilled-cheese sandwich. She brewed some of her mom's favorite herbal tea, then put the humble meal on a silver serving tray, and carried it to her mother.

She settled in a chair beside the bed and sipped her tea as Anne ate the meal with very little gusto.

"Mom, would you eat more heartily if I booted up the computer?" Katherine knew the answer before she asked.

"Well, it couldn't hurt. I'm just so excited about looking at the message and the websites."

Anne's eyes twinkled with a mischief that Katherine had not seen for some time, and she was thankful to see spirit back in her mom.

The computer booted up, and Katherine found the file with the e-mail message. She printed it out for her mother, then teased her by waving it in front of her and saying, "when you've finished all your meal, you may have it, young lady."

"Okay, I didn't want to do this, but I'm going to pull rank. I am your mother and your boss, so hand it over."

"Oh, all right, but you had better finish that meal anyway."

"My, I was out of the office just a few days, but you'd think I'd been gone a year."

Anne chuckled, and then her mouth dropped open.

"What is it, Mom? Is something wrong?"

"Was this code, this *IS4031*, on here last night?" Anne's voice became louder and more high-pitched as she spoke. "You didn't tell me about this."

"Yes, yes. I forgot about that. What does it mean? All I could think of was the verse out of Isaiah about the eagle. Do you think it could be related to that?"

"Oh, yes, that's exactly what it's related to. Whoever sent this must have known your father, and maybe me, personally."

Anne told Katherine the history of the eagle signal. "When your father was young, he was in a little club with the boys from his church. They wanted a secret code that had to be recited before they would let someone into their clubhouse. Their Sunday School teacher had just taught a lesson about the eagle and had asked the boys to memorize Isaiah 40:31. When they were deciding on a code, one of the boys suggested the verse. Well, they thought the verse was too long for a password, so they shortened it to IS4031. Some of the guys went all the way through high school and on to college together. They kept using the code for various things, and they introduced some of their new buddies to the code."

"Oh, my goodness! I think I know who sent the message. I can't remember his name, but I think I can find it."

"Mom, you have got to calm down...."

"Katherine, get on up to the attic and find a box marked *Barkley*. In it, I think we will find the name of the person who sent that e-mail. Hurry, and be careful. Here, take your cell phone with you. I don't want you to get stuck up there."

Katherine got her purse and got her cell phone out of it. She left the cordless phone on her Mom's bed so they could be in communication with each other.

"Okay, sweetheart, be careful – and travel on wings of eagles." Anne was so thankful that Katherine was with her when she remembered the origin of the Eagle Signal.

Anne felt younger than she had in years; she felt as though a weight had lifted off her shoulders. However, in some ways, she felt older and began to ponder what she might find out in the next few days and if she would want to know everything they found out about her husband's death so long ago.

CHAPTER TEN

KATHERINE stepped up the narrow stairway leading to the attic. In the dim light of the single light bulb, she caught her toe on the edge of the last step, tumbled through the attic door, and came face to face with a multitude of dust bunnies.

She surveyed the neatly stacked boxes that punctuated the attic space. So many rows of boxes were there. Where should she start? Just as well begin with the nearest and work her way around. She shifted each box in the first pile to check all sides, but found none marked *Barkley*. With dust-covered hands, she pushed and shoved each box to check every side. None had the label she searched for. Where could it be?

The phone rang. When she picked it up, her mother asked, "What's taking so long? The anticipation is killing me".

"I've checked every box up here and can't find it."

Anne described the box again.

"It's just not here, Mom".

Anne let out a long sigh. "Come on back. We'll look another day."

Back in her mother's bedroom, Katherine asked, "Mom, when was the last time that you saw that box?"

"I don't know. Webb took a lot of stuff to the attic when we moved in here from the last apartment. You know, now that you mention it, I don't know that I've seen that box since we left the first apart...."

Katherine could see in her mother's eyes that something had just hit her like a bolt of lightning.

"What is it, Mom? Do you remember something?" Anne's eyes had widened and she dejectedly threw her hands up in the air.

"I don't think I've seen that box since the first apartment. In fact, it may have been taken with the notes. Oh, dear. I can't really remember when I saw it last." Anne looked distressed.

"It's okay, Mom. We will just keep praying for revelation. I believe God is going to let us discover what happened to Daddy." Katherine was surprised to realize that she really *was* confident that God would provide the information. "For now, Mom, you've got to get some rest. We'll check out those websites later." Katherine's voice must have carried more authority that she thought, because Anne settled down.

After her mother drifted off to sleep, Katherine slipped into the kitchen and set up her laptop. She typed in the one of the web addresses, and... bingo! She was taken to the website of an atomic-bomb veteran.

Apparently, the government had assigned privates and corporals to secure the testing sites and to clean up the mess afterwards. This guy complained about the radiation exposure and wanted others to join him in a lawsuit. She would show this to her mom, but it did not look very promising.

The other website showed a little...well, a *lot* more promise.

There was no name on the site, but it showed a picture of an atomic test and gave information about the Van Allen rings – which form a magnetic field around the earth. When the bombs went off, they often reacted with the Van Allen rings. Initially the scientists wanted this to happen, but after a while, the rings did not react the same. The author of the website stated that this reaction caused the sky to catch on fire in April of 1962 and burned a hole in the ozone layer.

Katherine could hardly believe her eyes. Her dad had passed away in 1962. Could there be a connection between the two? Her mother's suspicions in living color sanctioned on that website. She scrolled down to the bottom of the page, looking for a contact email. None was listed, so she clicked on each tab and scrutinized every page. Still, she had no luck.

She bookmarked the web page and pondered over the latest development. If only they had the name of the person who sent the e-mail, but how could they get it?

Katherine was startled out of her daze by a call on her cell phone.

"Hello."

"Hello, Katherine. This is Jack Hancock. I hope I'm not disturbing you."

"Oh, no. It is good to hear your voice. What are you up to today?"

"I'm just tying up some loose ends at work before heading home in a few minutes. Hope you don't mind me calling."

"No, no. I'm glad you called."

"How's your mother?"

"She's sleeping right now. We've had a busy day, and she was all tuckered out."

"Do you think we could get together this weekend for dinner and/or a movie?"

"Jack, I really don't know. I want to see you, but I do not know about Mom's condition. Tell you what. I will have to go into work for a while Saturday. How about meeting me at the deli across the street for lunch? Say around *noonish*."

"That'll be great – but as soon as your mom gets better, I want to take you out for a real date."

"That sounds wonderful." Katherine was sure that the lieutenant could hear her heart beating wildly, though she tried to sound completely in control.

"I'll see you Saturday around noon."

"I look forward to seeing you, Jack."

"Me too. 'Bye for now."

"Bye-bye."

Katherine gave a little squeal when she hung up the phone. When she looked up, David stood in the doorway. Suddenly, the room seemed to heat up and she hoped her face had not turned bright red.

"'Bye for now, Lieutenant," David said good-naturedly, teasing his sister and tweaking her fire-engine-red hair.

"Oh, shush, Big Brother. Hey, have I got some news to tell you." Katherine's mind raced about their dad's death.

"You mean other than the fact that you and the military man are fast becoming a hot item?"

"Other than that, I mean about our dad – but I had better let Mom tell you herself. She's sleeping right now." Katherine loved holding her brother in suspense.

"You mean that there may have been problems with the A-bomb tests," David said, so nonchalantly that Katherine's feathers fell immediately. "How did you know?"

"I used to eavesdrop on Mom, Mary, and Webb. I've known about it a long time."

"Did you know about the Eagle Signal too?"

"No. What's the Eagle Signal?"

Katherine filled him in about the Eagle Signal and the mysterious e-mail. She pulled up the website again and they took time perusing it until they heard their mother stirring. They headed toward her room to discuss the day's events.

While they were talking, Katherine typed in the web address for the third time, and then printed out the information for her mother to read.

She printed out the information, and Anne began to cry when she read the copy. "This is what I've suspected for years. Your dad knew the tests affected the atmosphere, and he was afraid of this happening. When he died and I heard that others died also, I knew in my spirit that this was what happened." "David, Katherine...let's pray for revelation."

They heard a car pull up. Anne could see out her bedroom window that it was Mary Stennis.

"Let's wait for Mary. She knows about this, and young man," Anne said, pointing at David, "Mary will fix your little red wagon for eaves-dropping on us."

Anne smiled, so David knew he was not in too much trouble.

Once Mary joined them in Anne's room, they quickly filled her in, and she joined them in prayer.

They all knew the Lord had heard their prayer. The answer lay in His hands now.

Mary shooed David and Katherine out of the room, insisting that Anne must rest.

"Mary, please let me tell Mom one more thing." David playfully pushed against Mary's shoulder with his smiling all the while.

"All right, young man, but remember she just got home from the hospital."

"I just wanted to tell you that your daughter is being pursued by Lieutenant Hancock. They have a hot date for this Saturday."

"We have a lunch date," Katherine said, grinning, "but I must admit that I'm as excited as if we were going to the high school prom."

They all grinned too.

"Congratulations, sweetheart. I am so happy for you. You know I want the very best for both of my children. If this military man is the best, then let's pour on the prayers and ask the Lord to work this out. However, if he is not the best for my girl, then I want the Lord to block it as fast as He can." Anne knew the last part of her statement might not be what her daughter wanted to hear, but she would rather have Katherine be single and live in peace for the rest of her life, rather than marry the wrong person and live in misery."

"I know you want the best for me, Mom, but can we focus on the positive, just for now?" Katherine knew her mother's statement was wise, but …, she was still hopeful about Lieutenant Jack Hancock.

Chapter Eleven

On Saturday, Katherine dressed very carefully. She wanted to look stunning, yet understated. She tried on several outfits, decided on a floral dress, and accented it nicely with her favorite emerald earrings.

She spent several hours at the office and checked the clock every five minutes. When it was finally 11:45, she checked her lipstick and hair, and then headed out the door.

As she entered the deli just before noon, she spotted Jack in the back booth. He waved slightly and stood up, waiting for her to take her seat

"I hope you're hungry," Jack said, hoping he did not sound too nervous. "I've been checking out the menu, and everything sounds delicious."

"I *am* hungry – and everything they serve here is delicious."

They ordered, and when the food arrived, Jack said grace over it. Each of them was thankful to be with someone who did not object to praying or talking about the Lord. They spent the next hour or so talking and just getting to know more about each other. Katherine felt so at ease with Jack that she began to tell him bits and pieces about her dad.

"Katherine, do you think the Lord gave your design firm this job so you can get more information about your dad? I don't know if you'll find out any more about his death, but you may get some information about his job – things that will make you feel closer to him."

"I hadn't even thought about it. It could possibly be an answer to Mom's, Mary's, and Webb's prayers."

"Now I know your mom and Mary, but who is Webb?"

Jack sounded a wee bit jealous, and Katherine loved it.

"Webb is Mary's late husband – but I think God still answers people's prayers even after they are gone sometimes."

Jack looked relieved when Katherine explained who Webb was and he hoped that she did not notice. She did, but she was too wise to say anything.

"Do you have time to ride out to the base?" Jack asked. "I've got to go my office for a few minutes, and it's in the building where you'll be working. We could look around for a little while and pray over the project."

"Let me call Mom, and if David and Carol have the afternoon covered, then I'll go for a while."

She called her mom on the cell phone, and Carol answered. Katherine hoped Jack did not hear Carol squeal when she told her their plans.

"Yes, you go on and ride to the base with him. Anne and I will start the wedding plans while you're gone."

Katherine turned away from Jack and in a hushed voice said into the receiver, "Down, girl. It's just an afternoon ride."

"Whatever you say, Miss Katherine, but I know what I'm sensing here," Carol almost screamed, "and it's heavy-duty romance!"

"So it's okay if I go. I'll be back around...."

She looked at Jack, who mouthed, *Five-thirty*.

"Five-thirty. Can you handle Mom until then?"

"Stay as long as you like. The boys brought movies and popcorn, so we are here for awhile."

"Thanks Carol. Tell Mom when I'll be there."

"You know she and David are going to be excited," Carol returned before hanging up.

"Well, they've got it covered," Katherine told her new military *friend*. "Actually they will be there for awhile. The boys brought a movies and popcorn."

"Good deal. Let's go then."

The drive to the base was relaxing. Jack and Katherine chattered on about everything and nothing in particular. Just enjoying each other's company was enough for both of them.

48

They arrived at the gate, and Jack flashed his ID to the guy in the booth. Katherine's name was on the clearance list because of the design project.

As they entered the administration building, Katherine felt an eeriness that she could not explain. She figured it was just the excitement of the day, so she did not mention it to Jack.

They headed to his office, and he booted up his computer to check his messages. Katherine walked around looking at his collection of books, pictures, and sports equipment.

"I guess you guys are rather active out here." She gestured toward the assortment of golf clubs, tennis rackets, baseball mitt, and football.

"Yeah, you know what they say. You can tell a guy's age by the price tag on his toys." Jack shook his head as he looked around the room. "I guess I do have quite a few toys."

"I'm used to it. David has his own toys, as do Trey and Trevor. Carol and I give them a run for their money sometimes. We're pretty good at some of your games."

Jack could tell that Katherine was setting him up for something, and he took the bait.

"Oh, yeah! Well, maybe we should all set up a game and see how well you girls do."

"You're on. I'll set it up with David and Carol and get back with you." Katherine batted her eyelashes in an exaggerated fashion as she added, "I don't know if I can hold out for an entire afternoon of competition."

"Somehow I think I've been framed, but maybe I'm up to the contest."

"We'll see, Lieutenant, we'll see."

"Okay, I'm finished here, so let's go up to the third floor and look around."

CHAPTER TWELVE

JACK held the door open for her and motioned toward the elevator, which carried up them up, and when they stepped off, they headed toward the west wing. They arrived at the door that led to the old officers' suite, and Katherine shivered slightly. She felt that eerie feeling return.

"Is something wrong?" Jack asked, though the temperature felt fine to him. "Are you cold?"

"No, no. I am okay. It is just a little odd. It seems that the flippant phrase 'frozen in space' that was used earlier is coming back to haunt me."

"Yeah, I know what you mean, but Leslie does have a knack for dramatics. I don't think it will be that strange."

Jack tried to sound more confident than he felt.

The door unlocked with an echo, which added to the weightiness of the moment, and Jack pushed it open. They entered the suite, which did indeed look frozen in time. There were pencils and pads on the tables, old Styrofoam cups waiting to be filled with coffee, an emery board, and nail polish on the secretary's desk. They walked around, speechless, looking at old bookshelves, opening and closing drawers, not fully digesting anything.

"How did you get a key?" Katherine asked, wanting to have normal conversation in the midst of their invasion of the past.

"I borrowed one from Leslie after I made the date with you. I was praying that she would lend it to me, so I could make good on my promise."

Jack could not believe how easy it was to be honest with Katherine.

"Praying. Is that something you do often, Lieutenant?" Katherine asked, thinking they might as well get their beliefs out on the table now.

"Well, yes, it is. Very often. I accepted Jesus as my Lord and Savior some years ago, and I have a personal relationship with Him. My relationship with Jesus is the most important part of my life."

He was praying, as he said it, that Katherine was a believer as well.

"I'm relieved, Jack, because I could never date anyone who didn't have a relationship with Jesus. My relationship with Jesus is the most important part of my life too. When I saw your fish-symbol tie tack the first day we met, I figured either you were a Christian or had received the tie tack as a gift and did not know what it was. The more we talked, the more assured I became that you shared my beliefs – and I'm quite glad."

"I'm relieved too, Katherine. The day we met, I noticed all kinds of symbols in your office, and I figured you, your mother, or both had to be Christians."

Jack smiled easily, realizing that he had met the love of his life, since she shared his first love – Jesus Christ.

"We both are, and so are David, Carol, and Mary. Webb was also, but of course, he and my dad are with the Lord, now. I am very blessed to have so many believers around me. How about you? Are you from a family of believers?"

"No, I'm afraid not. My dad died when I was small. He was in the military and was killed in the line of duty; but to my knowledge, he did not know the Lord. My mother, however, did receive Christ a few years ago, so I do have a Christian mom.

"I met Jesus when I was in college. One of my ROTC buddies was in a small group called, the Navigators. I started going ot their Bible studies, and through studying the Word, listening to the speakers, and just from watching the lives of those folks, I decided that the Christian life was for me."

At first there was sadness in Jack's eyes as he spoke, but his spark returned when he mentioned the Navigators.

"You are kidding! I was involved with the Navigators when I was in college."

Katherine's heart beat wildly. Not only had the Lord crossed her path with a Godly man but one who had been discipled by the Navigators.

God's word is true, Katherine thought.

She was reminded of the verse, *Delight yourself in the law of the Lord, and He will give you the desires of your heart.*

Jack silently thanked the Lord for bringing him a quality Christian girl. *Lord, You are good, and You are faithful.*

"Let's just look around for a few minutes and you can get a 'feel' for the place and what needs to be done." Jack was a little nervous. He was not sure he was exactly following protocol to be there, but this was for Katherine.

They walked from office to office and Katherine made some mental notes. She pointed out a few things to Jack, but mostly just looked at work spaces that could have been very much like the one her dad occupied at one time.

"Are you okay, Katherine?" Jack sensed a somber mood coming over his lovely companion.

"Yes, I'm fine. It's hard to explain, but I can almost see my dad sitting at one of these desks. This really is a walk down memory lane. Only they are not my memories, but my parents' memories."

"I'm sorry. This may not have been a good idea." Jack was afraid that he had made a misstep by bring her up to the spaces that had been entombed for so long.

"No, no, it is fine. The firm has a job to do and now is as good a time as any to face the past that this reminds me of." Katherine was surprised at how odd this all seemed.

"Are you ready to go?" Jack was very concerned about Katherine and hoped the experience was not too overwhelming.

"Yes, and thank you for bringing me up to see the office spaces. Now I will have my bearings before I come to start on the project. It is fine, Jack, I mean it. Thank you for doing this for me." Katherine's genuine smile put Jack at ease.

"Well, shall we go on down, collect our things, and head to the parking lot?" Jack was ready to get out of there. The whole area was a little eerie to him, as well.

CHAPTER THIRTEEN

As Katherine and Jack were headed off the base, Katherine fished a small note pad out of her purse and jotted down a few things about the rooms that she had just seen. "I like to make notes to remind myself of details. I am already trying to envision how we can update those offices."

Jack smiled and said, "I can tell that you really like your work. Do you think you will want to work in the design industry until you retire?"

"Well, maybe. If I get married and have children, I would like to stay home while the children are little. I think if at all possible, a mom should stay home until they are ready for school." Katherine could feel her skin getting hot with embarrassment. Why in the world did she bring up children? Still, she had thought about what a great dad Jack would be.

"How many children would you like to have?" Jack asked the question rather easily amid Katherine's embarrassment.

"Oh, I would like to have two, maybe three. One might get lonely. I did worry David a lot by following him around when I was little. However, it has been nice having a brother all these years." Katherine was very sincere in mentioning her appreciation of her brother, David.

"What about you, Jack? How many children would you like to have?" Katherine hoped his answer matched hers in number.

"Oh, about the same as you want. I am an only child, so I know that it does get lonely. With my age and today's economy, I think two is a good number." Jack reminded her of her brother. Men seemed more objective and straightforward in their thinking than women did, at times.

As they rounded the last corner to leave the base, Katherine spotted some guys carrying bowling bags. "Is there a bowling league on base?"

"Not really, some of the guys just like to get together and go bowling. Do you like to bowl?"

"I love bowling! I was on a league in college, and it is my favorite sport. Well, after swimming and tennis, it is my favorite. Do you like to bowl?" Katherine was really hoping that Jack would answer, yes.

"As a matter of fact, I do like to bowl. I like it a lot. Would you like to go sometime?" Jack was very pleased that he had found something they could possibly do together.

"Yes, and there is a bowling alley not far from my mom's house. We have time if you would like to go tonight." Katherine had not been bowling in awhile, and she really wanted to unwind after all that had happened over the past few days.

"Yes, I would love to go. I have clothes in my gym bag that I can change into. Do you want to change?" Jack's voice trailed off. He was unsure how to handle taking Katherine by her house to change.

Katherine sensed his hesitation and said, "Tell you what, take me by the deli and let me get my car. Then follow me to Mom's. I have some clothes there. We can both change there. Then we can go bowling, you can bring me back to Mom's after we finish, and I will spend the night with her."

"Sounds like a plan to me."

When they arrived at Anne's, David, Carol, and the boys had just left. Katherine introduced her to Jack and pulled her mother aside. "Mom, do you feel okay enough for me to go bowling with Jack? It is okay if you don't, I will tell him that we will go another time."

"Yes, yes, I feel fine. You know I wouldn't mind having a couple of hours to myself. I love my grandboys with all my heart, but I will enjoy the peace and quiet for a little while. Go and have fun. I feel fine."

Katherine went into her old bedroom to change into jeans and a green pullover top. She decided to wear black leather flats and she put a pair of socks in her purse to wear with the hideous bowling shoes. That was the one thing about bowling that she did not like; the shoes. Oh well, the good thing about the shoes is that everyone else would be wearing the same ones.

When she went into the living room where Anne and Jack were talking, Jack let out a low whistle of approval and then turned red and quickly and apologized to Anne for being ill-mannered.

"Nonsense, Jack. My daughter is quite lovely. I appreciate you showing your admiration." Anne was smiling broadly, as she spoke to the nervous young man.

"Mom, do you need anything before I go?" Katherine was thinking maybe she should stay home with her mom and not go out at all.

"No, you two go and have a great time. I'll be fine until you return." Anne waved the two young folks off and settled into reading a novel she had wanted to read for quite some time.

CHAPTER FOURTEEN

AT the counter, they got the dreaded shoes and then headed to their lane. As they changed their shoes and selected their balls, Jack heard his name being called. He turned in the direction of the voice and a look of disbelief came across his face.

"Jack Hancock, you old rascal, I cannot believe my eyes. Am I really seeing my college sweetheart?" A perky blonde ran toward Jack and gave him a big (too big for Katherine's liking) hug.

Jack stepped back from the blonde lady rather quickly, but she just moved closer toward him and grabbed his arm (a little too tightly for Katherine's liking).

It is so good to see you, Jack. It has been way too long. I have missed you. How have you been?" The blonde was gushing over Jack and had not acknowledged Katherine's presence.

"I'm doing fine. I would like for you to meet Katherine Starling. Katherine, this is Tamara Hardy." Jack fidgeted as the two women appraised each other.

Katherine remembered her manners, "It is nice to meet you, Tamara. How do you two know each other?" Katherine was purposefully ignoring the fact that Tamara had referred to Jack as her college sweetheart.

"Oh, Jack and I were quite an item in college. Everyone thought we would get married, and I wouldn't even have to change my monogram; you know, Hardy Hancock." Tamara looked coyly at Jack, and Katherine felt her insides twist into a knot that would rival a seasoned sailor's handiwork.

Jack looked about as uncomfortable as a deer in headlights as the two women waited for him to speak.

About that time, a man who was talking to his child, absent-mindedly walked into Katherine who had just selected her bowling ball for the evening. As the man knocked Katherine off balance, the ball teetered for a moment and then fell from her grasp. She lunged forward trying to catch it, but instead, knocked into Tamara who had a drink in one hand and was 'pawing' Jack with the other one. Tamara's drink slipped out of her hand and onto a man seated behind her.

The ball skittered across the floor. Jack grabbed it before it could cause more trouble. The man who had been soaked by Tamara's drink jumped up and turned around, glaring at a shocked Tamara. He started to say something, but when he recognized the petite blonde, he clamped his mouth shut.

Katherine came to her senses and said, "Tamara, I am so sorry." Then after glancing at the man who was soaked from the unfortunate incident, she added, "Let me see if I can get some towels, Sir." Katherine took off to the front counter to see if they could help her.

Jack quickly put the ball back in the rack and took off to help Katherine.

Katherine had made it to the counter and the guy working there handed her the requested towels. Jack said from the end of the counter, "Kat, throw those to me and I'll take them back." She threw him the towels; he caught them, and turned to go help dry off Mr. Body Builder.

As Jack returned to the scene of the crime, he found Tamara and the guy laughing and talking like old friends. Jack gave him the towels and he began drying off, still talking to Tamara.

Tamara smiled and looked at Jack and said, "Jack, you are probably going to laugh about this. Do you remember when we were going together in college, and you did not want to go to the dance after homecoming?"

"Yes, I went to a Navigator camping trip. I left right after the game, and you said it was fine. You were going to the dance with your sorority sisters." As Jack was talking, he also remembered that it was the next week that Tamara had ended their relationship.

"Well, you are going to think this is funny. At the dance that night, I met Blaine, this Blaine." She emphasized the name *Blaine* and pointed at the guy who was still toweling off her big Slurpee sized drink.

Jack looked blankly for a moment and then realization hit him. "Oh, this is Blaine. I do remember, now." Jack then extended his hand and said, "How are you? It has been a long time."

"Yes, I remember you, now. Sorry for breaking you and Tamara up, back then. Blaine looked sheepishly at his feet for a moment.

"Don't mention it. I think life has a way of working out for the best." As Jack made that statement, he looked over admiringly at the still stunned Katherine.

"Well, Blaine and I started talking while you and Katherine went to the counter. We have both been married, have kids, and now we are both divorced. Isn't that interesting?" Tamara was talking to Jack but the object of her attention was clearly Blaine.

"Yes, that is so interesting." Jack nodded his head up and down, and Katherine could tell he was trying hard not to laugh.

"Well, Tamara continued her conversation, "I am going to drive Blaine home and get him all dry and warm. Maybe make him some hot cocoa or hot tea and make sure he does not catch his death of cold. We just cannot have that."

"You always took good care of me, Tamara. Why did I let you get away?" Blaine seemed sincere as he made that statement.

"Let's not worry about that now, Sweetums. Let's just get you home and get you all dry and warm. Tamara will take care of you."

"Katherine, don't you worry one bit about soaking down my Blaine, here. I'll take care of him. You two have a great time. Good to see you again, Jack. Bye now!" Tamara showed her flawless dental work as she smiled and left on Blaine's arm.

Jack shook his head back and forth a few times and then said, 'What just happened?"

Katherine laughed and replied with, "I have no idea, but I think my clumsiness just made a match." They both burst out laughing and sat down on the bowling seats.

The guy who had run into Katherine and caused the whole mishap, came over, "Miss, I am so sorry. My son had just asked to go to the re-stroom. He ate a hot dog and had a milk shake with it, against my better judgment. He was getting sick. I saw what happened, but saw that your husband was helping you. So, I took off to the restroom with my boy, afraid we'd have another mess if I didn't. Is everything okay?" The man looked genuinely worried.

"Yes, everything is fine. No one was hurt, just one guy got a little damp. Thank you for coming over. I hope your son is okay." Katherine was really concerned about the little boy.

"Oh, he's fine. Do you two have children? Well, that is none of my business, but if you do, you know what I am talking about. Kids are sick one minute and back bowling up a storm the next." He pointed toward their lane where his son was sending a granny bowl to the gutter. "He is not very good, but he has a great time, and that is what matters. Well, just wanted to check on you folks and extend my apologies for being clumsy.

As the guy made his way back to his family's lane, Jack said, "Well, are you up to bowling or has this experience tuckered you out?"

"Why Lieutenant Hancock, it would take more than this to 'tucker me out'. I can still hold my own in a round or two of bowling." Katherine playfully punched Jack on the arm as she got up to retrieve her bowling ball.

"Well, see if you can hang onto the ball, this time, Missy." Jack knew he was treading onto dangerous ground with his last statement.

"Oh, Jack Hancock, GAME ON; it is GAME ON!"

Katherine smiled as she challenged her handsome date and he smiled back; not caring if he was going to win or lose at bowling, but hoping to win his lovely companion's heart.

As the two waited for the pins to set-up for the first frame, they each wondered why they had not corrected Clumsy Guy when he had assumed they were a married couple. They also thought about the fact that the topic of children had come up twice in one day. Katherine then wondered if there were more 'Tamaras' in Jack's past, waiting to reappear. Jack wondered if he would have to further convince Katherine that she is now the lady who holds his interest.

CHAPTER FIFTEEN

JACK and Katherine entered Anne's living room still laughing from the night's events. Anne smiled at the young couple and said, "Well, looks like you two had a great evening. Come on into the kitchen. I have the fixings for s'mores. Who wants one?"

"Mom, I probably shouldn't. One of those this late will pack on the pounds." Katherine was suddenly feeling self-conscience. She had a good figure, but she knew she was not petite like Little Tamara, who had been Jack's dating partner for a while, and maybe he liked his women small.

"Well, maybe the Lieutenant would like to have one of my delectable treats." Anne completely ignored Katherine's protests and directed the question to Jack.

"Yes, ma'am! I would love to have one. This reminds me of my old camping days. We used to roast hot dogs and marshmallows. Then one of the guys' mom started sending chocolate bars and Graham crackers to go with the marshmallows. They are delicious." Jack felt a wave of nostalgia as he thought of his camping days.

Anne smiled and said "Well, let me go into the pantry and get all the ingredients. I will be right back."

"Are you sure you want to think about your camping days. After all, it was that fateful camping trip that caused your breakup with Tabitha, I mean Tamara." Katherine immediately hoped that Jack did not detect any jealousy in her little petty remark.

Jack gave a toothy grin and said, "No, I am grateful for that fateful camping trip. Tamara has her good points, but she is flighty, self-indul-gent, and you saw how fast she ditched me tonight for Blaine. Well, that was a flashback to what she did in college. She is all about what is best for Tamara. I hope she and Blaine make it this time, but my interests lie elsewhere."

Katherine smiled and Anne came back from the pantry with the s'mores' ingredients. "Mom, let me help you and I may just have one. Who wants to diet on Saturday night, especially tonight?" She flashed Jack one more grin and started helping her mom assemble the treats.

As they leaned on the counter and ate the wonderful sugary concoctions, Jack pulled his keys out of his pocket and said, "I am going to have to empty my pockets to make room for this wonderful treat. If I had on my sweatpants, I would keep eating, but I had better stop. Mrs. Starling, they were delicious and a perfect ending to a great evening. Thank you for your generosity.

"You are quite welcome, Jack, and you are welcome at my house anytime. I do hope to see you again, soon." Anne was very pleased with her daughter's new suitor and did hope he would be around their family for years to come.

Katherine picked up Jack's key ring and fingered a tiny odd-shaped key. "Jack, what does this little guy open? Not that it is any of my business; you do not have to answer that. He just looks very odd."

"Oh, he, err, it opens my new safe. I bought it a few weeks ago. My mom gave me my dad's class ring, gun, and a few other mementos, and I wanted to keep them secure. I put some important documents in there, as well. You know, it just pays to take extra measures sometimes." Jack did not seem to mind Katherine's prying question.

Anne put her hands on her head and said, "Safe, that may be where the box is, in the safe."

"Mom, are you talking about the safe in your bedroom or the one at the office, and what box, the Barkley box?"

Katherine was unsure of what her mother was talking about.

Chapter Sixteen

"Of course, that must be where the box is, in the safe. After I started planning to build the house, Webb insisted that I put in a hidden safe. He had taken some documents and other things and hidden them in he and Mary's home, but he knew that eventually I would need to have possession of them. That is when he suggested that I have a hidden safe put in when the house was built." Anne had not thought about the safe since she and the children had moved into the place, years ago.

"Mom, I never knew there was a hidden safe. Where is it?" Katherine thought she knew every nook and cranny in the house. She was shocked to find out there was a hidden safe. What else was in this house, a hidden staircase like the one in an old Nancy Drew novel?

"It is in the attic. You were very close to it when you scourged around up there the other day. It never occurred to me that it might be there. Do you think you could look tonight, Katherine, or is it getting too late?" Anne was hoping Katherine would agree to look tonight.

"Yes, I will look tonight. I want to see if the box is there, too. Where is the safe, Mom? I did not see anything unusual, and I thought I looked everywhere up there?" Katherine was trying to figure out where the safe could possibly be.

"You know where the big built-in bookcase is at the end of the room, it is in between some of those shelves. That is why I keep the old encyclopedias there, to camouflage it. Well, actually that was Webb and Mary's idea, but I have never moved them, have never thought about it, actually." Anne was getting very excited at the prospect of finding the box.

Jack had been quietly listening to the two women discuss the attic safe, and finally broke the silence with, "Would you ladies mind filling me in on this mystery or is it something you want to keep secret?"

Katherine looked at her mom to make the decision on this and Anne answered with, "Oh, Jack, I'm sorry we must have sounded like we were talking in circles. I am trying to solve the mystery of my late husband's death, and we think some clues, or maybe even the answer may be in a box that I last saw in the apartment where we lived when David passed away. That box may very well be in the hidden safe."

Katherine then said to Jack, "Jack, I know it is getting late, so I will stay here with Mom and go up to the attic. You must be tired, so you can go on home and get some rest. I will walk you to the door..."

Jack cut her sentence off and said, "Not so fast, Miss Starling. If it is okay with you and your mom, I would love to go up to the attic and help you look for the hidden safe. I love a good mystery, and this sounds quite interesting."

"That is not necessary, Jack, but if you don't mind, I would feel safer with you going up to the attic with Katherine. The bookcase is at the end of the room. The safe has not been opened for years. That reminds me; I have to go and find the key." Anne headed in the direction of her bedroom, determined to find the key that could unlock this mystery.

"Then it is settled, I am going up to the attic with you, Madam. I know you are capable of doing this on your own, but I do love an opportunity to help a beautiful damsel in distress. It is not often that I get to slay a dragon for a lady." Jack felt a little silly with what he had just said, but he really did not care; he wanted to slay this dragon for Katherine and her whole family, and maybe for himself, as well.

Katherine batted her eyelashes at Jack and then curtsied, "Then I just might start calling you, Prince Charming."

Jack laughed, bowed, and helped his damsel back to her standing position.

CHAPTER SEVENTEEN

"HERE it is. I am so glad I found it, it was taped underneath the top of one of my dresser drawers." Anne seemed as giddy as a schoolgirl as she handed the key to Katherine.

"Now you two put that in a safe place, so it does not get dropped, take a cell phone, flashlight, and you may want something to push back any cobwebs, dust, or whatever else may have found its way in that corner over the years." Anne laughed at the last part of her statement. "Don't worry, Katherine, I am sure there is nothing alive up there, except maybe a spider or two."

"Mom, you know I hate spiders." Katherine gave a moaning sound at the thought of the disgusting creatures.

"Mrs. Starling, I will take care of any creepy crawlies and get to your hidden safe. I will also keep your daughter safe during this mysterious expedition." Jack smiled warmly at Mrs. Starling thinking to himself, this lady would make a great mother-in-law and grandmother…

"Okay then, 007, let's get moving and find out what is in the attic. Here, put the key in your pocket, my cell phone is in mine, we need a flashlight and a feather duster." Katherine located a flashlight in one of the kitchen drawers, and Jack told her to not worry about a feather duster, he would personally manhandle any cobwebs they encountered.

"Katherine, call me on my cell phone if you need me." Anne wanted to be sure to get her call, no matter where she might be in the house at the time of the call.

"Will do, Mom." With that, Katherine and Jack started climbing the steps to the attic. "Okay, it is up two flights of stairs. Do you think you are up to this, Lieutenant? Katherine threw Jack a smile as she asked her question.

"I think I can muster up the energy for two flights of stairs, Miss Starling." Jack was enjoying the banter between he and his crimson haired date.

As they entered the attic, Katherine turned on the light switch and there it was at the end of the room, the bookcase. Katherine had not even paid it any attention as she had rummaged through the boxes during her earlier visit. Now she could plainly see the encyclopedias that must be shielding the hidden safe.

They hurried over to the bookcase and Jack removed a couple of cobwebs, however, the dust was not too bad for years of neglect. He removed several of the books and there was no safe. He removed more of the books and still no safe. He was getting worried and then it occurred to him to feel the panel of wood. He ran his hand around the wood, putting a little pressure on it, and then it popped open. There tucked neatly in the wood was the safe. However, on the safe was a combination lock. Jack stated flatly to Katherine, "Uh oh, Houston, we may have a problem."

"What, what's the problem." Katherine could not see the safe because Jack was positioned in front of it, but she so hoped they could get into it. If they couldn't, her mother would be devastated.

"We need a combination. I have a feeling the key is for after we get into the safe. The documents may be in a lockbox. Call your mom and ask her if she has any idea where the combination may be." Jack was hopeful that they could get into the safe.

Katherine excitedly punched her mom's number into the phone. Her mom answered and Katherine asked her about the combination.

"She's going to look in the dresser where she found the key. She said she felt some paper there but was going to look later." Katherine was so afraid the paper might not produce the needed combination.

Katherine could hear her mom fumbling with the dresser and she heard paper rustling. "Katherine, I found the paper. There are numbers on here. Are you putting them in?"

"No, Jack is, here he is, tell him the combination."

Katherine held the phone to Jack's ear and he followed the numbers as Anne read them out to him. When the last number was put in, the safe opened. Jack and Katherine jumped a little and then laughed. Katherine put the phone to her ear and said, "Mom, it worked, the safe opened. We will be down in a few minutes with the contents."

Jack gathered up the contents and there was a lockbox in the safe. "Let's let your mom unlock it. She has been waiting all these years, it seems fitting to let her be the one to open it."

Katherine's heart melted at the unselfishness in Jack's statement. Many people would have wanted to see what was in a mysterious lockbox, but he knew that the right thing to do was let her dad's widow have that honor. "I agree that it is fitting to let Mom be the one to open this."

Jack quickly closed the safe, put the books back, and they both gathered up the safe's contents to take down to the anxious Anne.

"Here it is, Mom, I think this is what you have been waiting for." Katherine could hardly contain her excitement as she sat the lockbox in her mom's lap.

Jack handed Anne the key and she put it on the lockbox and asked them to have a seat. Katherine and Jack sat across from Anne and wondered what she was about to say.

"I called your brother and asked if he wanted to come over to see what is in the box. He said he could not come tonight but he would like to be here when the box is opened. So, here is what we are going to do. We will all go to church tomorrow, then go out to eat for a quick lunch, we will then come here and open the box, together."

"Okay, Mom. I am very disappointed that we cannot open it now, but I do understand. Dad was David's dad too, and he has a right to be here. However, we could open it now and just act surprised tomorrow. David won't know the difference." Katherine was half-kidding, but she really wanted to know what was in the box.

"No, I am tempted to do that. However, let's wait until your brother can be here. You know he would find us out, anyway. Carol will not be here. She and the boys are going to her folks' after church. Her Uncle Ralph and Aunt Dorothy are here from Illinois, and Carol wants to spend time with them. She sends her love and hopes that we find what we are looking for in that box. I may call Mary and see if she wants to come. She and Webb are the reason we have that safe. She needs to be here, as well."

Katherine looked at Jack and said, "Jack, you come and be with us. You helped us tremendously tonight. Mom can vouch for me when I tell you that I am not good with combination locks. My high school principal had to use his bolt cutters more than once on my locker. He finally had me leave the combination in the office, so I wouldn't keep having to buy new locks. If you had not been here tonight, I would probably still be up there trying to get it open."

"Yes, Jack, please come and join us tomorrow. Also, thank you so much for what you did tonight. I can verify that Katherine is combination lock challenged. You were a big help to us tonight and I thank you so much. Please be our guest tomorrow." Anne really hoped that Katherine's new friend would accept her invitation.

"Thank you both for the invitation. I would accept, but my mother's birthday was several days ago, and I am going to church with her and then taking her to lunch. If I cancelled on her at this late date, I would surely go into the dog house for quite awhile."

"That is interesting that your mother's birthday was this past week. Mine was on the 22nd, when was your mom's."

"The 22nd, wow, you and she have the same birthday. Well, I will tell her that she has a birthday twin." Jack was thinking that maybe he would have to juggle the two ladies birthdays next year. This could be interesting.

"Well, please tell my birthday twin, happy birthday. I hope you both have a wonderful time."

"Yes, Jack, please tell her happy birthday from the Starling family. Hopefully, we will get to meet her, soon." Anne was already planning an upcoming meal with Jack and his mom as their guests.

"I will tell her. Thank you again for inviting me for tomorrow's meal and the opening of the mysterious lockbox. I do wish that I could be here, but I wish you the very best."

"We understand, Jack." Katherine took Jack's arm as they walked toward the door. I hope you have a wonderful time with your mom tomorrow.

"Thank you for understanding, and I will call you later to hear what mysterious items are lurking in the lockbox." Jack stated that while doing a poor impression of Count Dracula that made Katherine laugh.

"Well, good night, Princess Katherine. I had a really good time." He bowed and moved to open the door.

Katherine curtsied and said, "Thank you for a most enjoyable evening, Prince Charming."

Chapter Eighteen

After church the next morning, Anne, Katherine, David, and Mary all went to a restaurant for lunch. Neither of them ate very heartily because they were so excited about getting back to Anne's and discovering the contents of the lockbox. Upon leaving the restaurant, they headed to Anne's hoping to find out more information about David Sr.'s death.

"This is it." Anne had opened the lockbox and there was the box marked, Barkley. "This is the box that you were looking for the other day, Katherine."

David could hardly contain his curiosity as he waited for his mom to open it. "Mom, what's in the box that is so incredible?"

"Well, let's see…"

Anne pulled out old photographs, receipts, a rough drawing of a house plan.

"This was to be our house after your dad finished the assignment and we were to be relocated. When I had *this* house built, I went by this plan from memory. David, how did I do?"

"Pretty good. Did Dad draw this plan?"

"Yes, he did. We used to sit in that little bitty apartment and dream of the day when we would have a larger house."

Anne sighed, thinking of days gone by, and then reached into the box.

"Here's what we've been looking for – the *Eagle Signal* file. Your dad put this together in case anything ever happened to him. I was so upset when he died that I never got around to looking for it."

Mary interrupted Anne and said, "After the break-ins, Webb took all of this to our place, then later put it in the lockbox, and then the hidden safe. You remember how protective he was, and he wanted to help keep you all as safe as possible." Mary's eyes were misting up as she spoke of her late husband.

Anne reached out and patted Mary's hand in sympathy, then continued her thoughts about those days. "You see, your dad knew the atmosphere was taking a beating from the atomic testing, and he knew that the government was trying to blame it on spray products – Freon and such. He and everyone involved in the projects knew that it was really atomic bombs. David used to say, 'Just think about it. Which do you think affects the ozone layer more, a big bomb being set off into it or you spraying your armpits miles and miles away from it?'"

Very carefully, Anne opened the IS4031 file. In it were reports of fiery reactions in the sky and how the officials were working to cover up the damage being done.

Anne searched for a letter to David's friend, but it was nowhere to be seen.

"David kept copies of everything he wrote about this issue, but the letter isn't here, and I can't remember the guy's name."

As she continued looking, David and Katherine began reading the reports.

"It sounds like to me that Dad was planning to get out of the atomic testing program," David said.

"He was. As soon as his contract ran out, he was going to join an architectural firm. The plan was that eventually we would have our own firm with me helping with paperwork and decorating. We never got to that point. That is why I took the life-insurance money, opened Starling Designs, and saw to it that you two went to college. He would have been happy with those choices."

Anne eyes had been misty since Katherine set the box in her lap, and her voice still wavered with emotion.

"Now I believe more than ever that David was murdered and that someone out there knows about it. I think a lot of people know, and I also believe that others were killed. The questions are, how do we find these people, and what do we do with this information?"

As she spoke, Anne reminded the others of a scared little girl.

"Annie, you have come through too much to get scared now," Mary said with deliberate frankness. "I'll tell you what we are going to do. We are going to pray for continued revelation. We are going to pray not to be embittered over the situation and ask for God's grace and guidance every step of the way. Your parents, Webb, and David would be very proud of you. I think they may be looking down on us right now, cheering us on to victory. What we have here today is a victory. We have won many battles, but the war is not over, not yet. We are going onward – onward, Christian soldiers."

Katherine broke out in a chorus of that very song, and the rest of the group joined in. They felt God's mercy and grace pouring out in that moment. They knew that He would see them through the days ahead and that God's divine guidance would answer their many unanswered questions.

Several states away, a lone computer operator had his head bowed low in prayer for David Starling's widow. He asked the Lord to reveal information to her that would lead her to the truth about her husband's death and for guidance to use that information in a mature, Godly manner.

He asked for restoration for David's family. He asked for guidance for himself, for the courage to step out on faith and help them unlock the secrets to this tragic event.

CHAPTER NINETEEN

O N Monday morning, Katherine rode out to the base to begin working on the design project. She checked in with the secretary who told her to head on up to the offices that were to be renovated.

She arrived at the suites, where a security guard let her in. She started going from office to office making notes and taking measurements. Before she knew it, it was almost noon. She decided to take a break and then come back after lunch and finish her work.

She went down to her car and leaned her head back on the seat to collect her thoughts for a few moments. A tapping startled her at her window. She sat up and smiled when she saw Jack. She motioned for him to join her.

He strode around the car like a proud peacock and settled in on the passenger side.

"I didn't expect to see you this early," she said. "What's going on?"

"We got out of the meeting early, and I'm headed to the commissary for lunch. Would you like to join me?"

"Yes, I am taking a break and was going off base for lunch, but I would rather dine with a handsome lieutenant. Do you know if one is available?" Katherine gave Jack's arm a playful squeeze as she joked with him.

Katherine filled him in on their findings in the lockbox.

"That's incredible, Kat. I hope you and your family find out everything there is to know about your dad's death."

"Yes, I do hope we are headed to the climax of the story. It would bring much needed closure to all of us."

"I hope not the climax of our relationship." Jack looked very serious as he made that statement.

"Now you hold on just a minute, mister! Why in the world would you suggest such a thing?"

The fiery redhead's eyes misted over as she waited for a response.

"Well, I keep thinking about how we met and how our meeting has helped to unfold the mystery about your dad's death, and I can't help worrying that maybe it's the only reason that we met."

Jack stopped speaking. He did not trust his voice to say anything more.

Katherine's heart melted as she looked at the uniformed man sitting beside her.

"You can't mean that, Jack. Surely, the God we serve is so multidimensional that He could design our meeting to accomplish more than one purpose. I do not know where our relationship is going, but I am certainly not ready for it to be over. Let us not worry about it. We'll just let God unfold our relationship the way that He sees fit."

Now it was Jack's turn to feel his heart melting. He really hoped that Katherine was the one, and he would work on trusting God with their relationship.

"I agree, now, let's go get some lunch, Miss Starling."

"Don't mind if I do, Lieutenant."

CHAPTER TWENTY

KATHERINE finished her lunch with Jack, and as she was about to go and finish taking measurements and notes about the job, her phone rang.

"Hello."

"Katherine, its Mom." Anne's voice had an excited ring to it. "Are you sitting down?"

"Yes. What is it?"

"I just talked with Mary, and she checked my e-mails at the office. Guess who sent a message."

"Your friend from Mobile?"

"Yes! This time he gave his name – Nathan Parker. I knew immediately when Mary said his name. He wants to meet with us and tell his side of the story. He did indicate in the message that David was murdered and that he has known about it all these years but couldn't contact me."

"Who is he, Mom? How do you know this man?" Katherine had never heard of this man; how did her mom know him?

"Nathan was one of your father's roommates in college. They became very good friends and they went into the military when they graduated."

"Well, when is he coming? Did he give any more information?"

"He's coming tomorrow. Mary emailed him and gave him my phone number. We just talked long enough to set-up the meeting. I told him someone would pick him up at the airport, and we will all have dinner together. I reserved a hotel room for him."

"How is he getting here so fast?"

Katherine could not believe how quickly it was all unraveling.

"He's still in the service, and he has some work that he can do for this base here, so his trip is on the military. Poetic justice, don't you think?"

Anne thought it was the least that the government could do for her David and all the others who lost their lives in '62.

Katherine suddenly remembered that her mother was still recuperating, and she did not want her to have to go back into the hospital.

"Mom, are you okay? I don't want you to get too excited."

"I'm fine, Kat. I am better than I have been in a long, long time. To think that in a few hours we are going to know the truth about your dad's death makes me feel like a teenager. God has heard our prayers, Katherine."

"I agree, Mom, I most certainly agree!"

Katherine hardly remembered the drive home as she thought about Jack, Nathan Parker, and her dad. Her head was almost spinning as she pulled into her driveway.

CHAPTER TWENTY-ONE

NATHAN Parker's plane was to arrive at 10:00 A.M. They all piled into David and Carol's van. Jack had offered to go, though he said it would be hard to get away from the base. Katherine assured him she would be surrounded by supporters, but he was expected to meet them for dinner.

"Nathan is going to stay at a hotel tonight. Then tomorrow afternoon he will report to the base to sign some papers, and the military will fly him home on one of their jets. Apparently, sometimes they fly their men one-way on commercial flights. Nathan said it saves them money, but you probably know that. I am rambling because this is rather exciting."

"I know you are all excited. I am looking forward to meeting everyone for dinner. This will definitely be one interesting meeting." Jack was happy for Katherine and her family. He hoped and prayed that they would receive closure concerning Katherine's father's death.

The plane arrived on time, and they waited nervously as the passengers came into the airport. A stocky man with a laptop was almost the last one into the concourse. He and Anne recognized each other almost instantly and waved at each other.

The entourage headed toward the man, and Anne made introductions. David helped Nathan with his luggage, and they all walked toward the parking lot.

"I'm so glad to see you again, Anne, and to meet your children and grandchildren. I know David would be so proud of all of you."

Nathan could hardly believe that he was with David's widow and children. He was here to do a job that had been nagging at him for a long, long time. He was here to right some wrongs and lay some issues at rest.

"Nathan, we're going to take you to our favorite restaurant for lunch. Then we want you to tour the design firm and David's architectural firm. Then we will take you to the hotel to rest, and someone will pick you up for dinner, which will be at the finest restaurant in town. I think this occasion calls for a grand meal in grand surroundings. After that, we'll began to unravel the mysteries that have hung over us for years."

Anne spoke with such authority that Nathan did not know what to say.

"Mister Parker, don't worry," David said. "Mom's bark is much worse than her bite. Just do what she says, and everything will be all right."

He hoped that his mother's good mood from the day before was still with her and that she would take his good-natured kidding in stride as usual.

"That's right, Nathan," Anne piped. "Just do as I say, and you won't get hurt."

She loved looking at Nathan. He reminded her very much of David. They were the same age, and their lives intersected in so many ways – college, military, and love of sports. Yes, Nathan's presence was stirring memories that Anne had thought were long gone.

"Well, okay, Mrs. Starling. Anything you say. Just as long as I have the privilege of visiting with this fine family for a couple of days. It's time to get some things out in the open and let you good people have closure to some issues."

They all sensed his sincerity in wanting to make things right.

"For starters, Nathan, call me Anne – or if I remember correctly, you and David called me, Annie. Let us not be formal. "Anne beamed as she spoke with her friend of days gone by. "This is really a happy occasion. The truth is going to be revealed, and then we are going on to the next chapter. God is answering many prayers with your visit."

"All right, Anne...er, Annie, I'll try to relax. I just feel that...that...."

He was overcome by emotion and could not complete his sentence.

"Tell you what, Nathan. We are almost to the restaurant. We are going to have small talk about our families, friends, churches, and we are not going to mention the heavy stuff until after dinner tonight."

Anne smiled as she spoke, and Nathan sensed a sincerity that he did not experience often in his circles...well, except at his church.

"My church is really the most important part of my life," he explained, "except for Jesus, of course. He has put me into a fellowship that is a source of encouragement and support. I don't think I would survive without them."

Nathan went on to tell them about the various departments and ministries of his church and some things about his job. His family was scattered, both parents dead, but he did have pictures of nieces and nephews to show off.

Anne, Katherine, and David shared with him about the two businesses that they headed up and about their church. Of course, Anne's grandsons took turns telling funny stories about school. They spent a couple of hours taking Nathan on a tour of the businesses, then a driving tour of the city, and finally dropped him off at the hotel so he could unwind before the evening meal.

As they drove out of sight, Nathan sighed a prayer of thanks for Anne and her family. They seemed as genuine as he remembered she and David being all those long years ago. He smiled to himself as he headed to his room.

The van was quiet for a few moments before David began praying, thanking the Lord for miraculously drawing their paths across Nathan's. He prayed for tonight's meeting and asked for special protection and provision for Nathan. The van was again silent as each sat alone in his or her thoughts.

David and Carol dropped Anne, Mary, and Katherine off at Anne's, then headed home.

"David, we'll go by and get Nathan," Anne said. "We're a little closer to the hotel. We will see you tonight, and be very careful. My grandsons ...well; all of you are precious cargo."

Anne felt overwhelmed with love for her son and his family.

"We'll be very careful, Mom, and we'll see you all tonight."

He, Carol, and the boys waved as they drove out of sight.

Mary and Katherine went to the design firm to check on phone calls, memos, and the latest assignments. Katherine also called Jack and double-checked with him on their meeting time.

It was decided that she would ride with her mother and Mary to take Nathan Parker to the restaurant. Then Jack would drive her to her own home. There were many things that she wanted to discuss with him, and she could check on her mother afterward. She had a feeling that Nathan and "Annie" had a lot of talking to do.

Anne walked through her home in a daze. She was thinking of days gone by, of what Nathan might or might not tell them, and of her dear David.

Oh, how I miss him.

Maybe tonight would bring closure. Although she would always love David, she knew that she and her children needed to put to rest the issues surrounding his death.

Anne finally decided to lie down and rest. She dozed off. She heard bombs exploding, and heard David calling to her.

She woke with a start and headed to the shower. Maybe after tonight she would have peaceful rest. She asked God to give her a calm spirit for tonight's meeting.

Chapter Twenty-Two

THE time arrived to pick up Nathan. Anne had dressed very carefully for tonight's meeting, choosing a teal suit with a floral scarf to match, her most elegant earrings, and a small circular brooch. Mary and Katherine also looked very sophisticated for the evening as they headed out the door and toward truth.

Nathan looked very handsome in a tweed sports jacket and khaki pants. He hardly ever wore anything but casual wear, but this was a special occasion. He had not been able to attend his friend's funeral, and in a way tonight, he was saying good-bye to his long-lost pal.

He waited in the lobby until the women pulled up to the door. A few moments passed before anyone spoke.

"You ladies look wonderful. I know this will be a very special evening," Nathan said sincerely, very pleased to be the escort of such a stunning group.

"You look very dapper, Mister Parker," Katherine responded.

"Well, this is a very important event. Something I have waited for, really only dared to hope for."

"Nathan, we are very grateful that you came all this way and are so willing to share your information," Anne told him.

"David Starling was the best friend I've ever had except for Jesus Christ, and I'm here for my dear friend."

They arrived at the restaurant, where David, Carol, the boys, and Jack were waiting.

It was evident to everyone that Jack only had eyes for Katherine, and those eyes were full of admiration. The waiters had situated them in a back room that had a larger table and lots of privacy. When they were all seated, David ordered appetizers for the group.

Even though it was a rather fancy restaurant, they prided themselves on the best iced tea in the city. A large pitcher of the coveted beverage was placed at each end of the table. Everyone was given a menu, and they took time to decide what they wanted. Soon the waiters took their orders.

Then Nathan said, "I can hold it no longer. I must tell you what I know about David's death."

All attention at the table turned to him.

"You all know that David designed launch vehicles for Intercontinental Ballistic Missiles (ICBMs) and lunar rockets. Well, that is what he had been assigned to do. He and I always kept each other posted on our secret assignments, I think for safety, peace of mind...well, I'm not really sure why, but we did. I knew that David was involved in atomic testing, and I was always concerned about his safety. He said not to worry, that his life was in the hands of Someone bigger than all of us, but I knew there was a lot of potential for something to go wrong with the tests."

Nathan's audience was hardly breathing, no one wanting to miss a word of what he was saying.

"I was on several test teams myself, and I know how they handled these things. They would fly us to New Mexico – you know, Roswell and Alamogordo – and do the practice tests. They have deserts that will never be habitable because of all the radiation. Then they would fly us to islands at night; sometimes blindfold us so we would not be responsible for knowing where we were and to make sure the locations did not leak out to the public.

"Oh, yes, the men were always from different places. There would be some from New York, Massachusetts, Ohio, others from California, Arizona. They would put the top guys from different areas on a team. Over the years, I have come to believe that this was for protection. If something went wrong and ten or twenty people from the same area were killed or injured, then the government would have some explaining to do, but if the guys were from all over, who was going to track it down?"

The waiters brought everyone's meals, and they ate slowly, listening to Nathan's story.

"Well, a month or so earlier, an evacuation team had probably gone in and relocated the natives to Hawaii or some adjoining island. This took place on a little island in the South Pacific. Then the evacuation team would build houses and other structures, cars and trucks were flown in, and a little village was set up. This would be the test site. When the bombs went off, the scientists and engineers would record the extent of damage. I always thought it was unnecessary, because everything was going to be annihilated anyway."

"This particular test was very important to Washington. It had to be kept completely quiet, because we were under a test-ban agreement with Russia, and if they found out that we were testing anyway...well, you can imagine what could have happened. Only the top guys were used, and David and Katherine, your dad was a top guy. He knew the importance of keeping our country's weaponry top-notch. He did what he did for the safety and security of this country, not to mention the safety and security of his family."

Nathan stopped for a moment to give everyone an opportunity to absorb the magnitude of what he was saying.

"David was not happy about being away from his family on Easter weekend, but he knew if this assignment was successful, he would be up for a promotion that would take all of you to California. He decided that he could sacrifice Easter with his family to get a better job that would lead to better benefits. Annie, you remember that David had been stationed in Kansas, and he would fly there and leave you and the children behind. I do not know if you knew it, but he demanded this because he wanted to be assured of your safety.

"This particular assignment was hard for him. He wanted to get out of the weaponry division and certainly the atomic division. He understood the philosophy behind the atomic bomb, but he did not agree with it. After you have seen the aftermath of those test sites, you don't want to be a part of it any longer."

Nathan paused and drank some of his iced tea, more to collect his thoughts than anything else.

"Nathan, if you want, we can stop for a while" Anne said, "I know this must be very taxing on your emotions."

As much as she wanted to get the story out in the open, she was more concerned with her husband's best friend's welfare. He looked tired, and she could only imagine the price that he had paid in carrying this story for so many years.

"It's okay, Annie. Let's continue while I still have my nerve up." Nathan smiled weakly. "As I was saying, the security of this particular assignment was very important, because President Kennedy had signed a test-ban agreement with Russia. Well, something had begun to happen in the atmosphere that did not bother everyone at first, but looking back, we should have been greatly alarmed.

"There is a magnetic field that surrounds the sun called the 'Van Allen Rings.' Scientists thought we could use this field to enhance the power of the atomic bombs, but what began to happen after so many tests was that the field began to react with the bombs, and extra sparks could be detected on test films. No one was alarmed until that fateful Easter weekend in sixty-two."

Nathan reached across the table and took Anne's hand. "Do you want me to continue? I know this is very hard for you."

She took a deep sigh and straightened her shoulders. "Nathan, I have to hear the truth. We all have to hear it, and you have to tell it. Please continue. I'm okay."

Chapter Twenty-Three

"WELL, I guess so many bombs and rockets had been sent into the atmosphere by this time that the odds were set against these guys. Not only was the atmosphere out of balance, but the bomb detonated just a little too early. Now this had happened before and usually was not a big deal, but on this day when the bomb went off, I guess it was at just the right angle to react in a catastrophic manner with the Van Allen Rings – 'a perfect storm situation' - and the sky caught on fire."

It was completely quiet for a moment.

Then, in unison, the grandsons said, "Wow!"

"Yeah, wow. That is what all the scientists and engineers thought. *Wow, how are we going to put out a fire in the sky?* Well, they did all they knew to do, and that was to radio Washington. The head of the team put in a call to D.C., and they got Vice President Johnson on the line. He told them not to worry, that he would inform the President, and they would figure out what to do, and he would get back with them. They waited for word from Washington, and no call came.

"Eventually the fire went out, and a helicopter appeared. They thought it was their rescue, but then they realized that there were two pilots in what they thought was a rescue helicopter. However, one pilot got in the helicopter that had brought them to the island. They thought maybe he was checking it, so they started gathering up their things. Then the guy in the 'rescue' helicopter started taking off, and then, so did the guy in their helicopter. You can imagine that the guys were stunned. At first, they did not know what was going on, and they tried Washington again, but no one would talk with them. They realized that they were being left on the island for some reason."

Nathan stopped for another sip of tea, and everyone was drying his or her eyes. They could all imagine their husband and father on that island, stranded and desperate to get home.

How could this have happened? Katherine thought. *You hear of things like this only in the movies.*

After a moment, Nathan continued his story, "The radio operator in the group started trying to just pick up signals. He finally got some guys in Australia, and they came and got them. Pictures of the fiery circle were taken, and the scientists and engineers diagrammed the circle and got an approximate estimate of its size. The Australia team flew them to a base in Hawaii, and some of the pilots there took them to the mainland.

"Of course, Washington said it was a fluke. There were also rumors that the pilot that left the island was never heard from again. There were reports in Hawaii about a helicopter being shot down over the Pacific that day, but no official announcement was ever made."

"It was the next week when I heard about David's death, and I saw a folder with his name on it marked *P-13*. Everyone in our division knew that was a code that meant *no questions were to be asked*, and whatever the government said happened, that was what you were supposed to believe."

"It was also around that time when we began to hear stories about the dangers of aerosol sprays and Freon. Well, I just have a hard time believing that something I spray on my armpits in my bathroom, miles below the ozone layer, is going to have more of an effect on the atmosphere than a bomb going off directly *in* the ozone layer."

Nathan stopped when he saw Annie smiling. "David used to say that, didn't he?"

He suddenly remembered the origin of the armpit statement that he thought of every time the EPA hollered about the effects of aerosols on the environment.

"The administration at that time was heavily involved in the space race, and I guess they felt if stories like this got out, there would be an outcry from the American public. In addition, there was the fact that we were under a test ban, and the administration kept ordering that the military continue with secret tests. If Russia had found out, we could have had an uprising from them."

"So what is the bottom line, Nathan?" Anne asked, already knowing but needing to hear Nathan say it.

CHAPTER TWENTY-FOUR

David took a deep breath and whispered a prayer before he made his next statement. He knew what he had to say would be painful, but it had to be said to bring forth the truth, closure, and he hoped eventual healing for all concerned.

"Annie, David was murdered. They all were. Some were made to look like suicides, some homicides, car wrecks, a number of things, but it was all murder – espionage. I am so sorry that it happened, and I am sorry that it took this long for me to find you. I really believe it was the hand of God that brought us together. He knew how much you and your children needed to know this, and He knew how I longed to tell you."

"When did you figure this out?" David asked, having a hard time believing the man's story though he knew it must be true.

"Right after my superior officer suspected that I had seen the folder, I was relocated overseas. I tried to contact you as soon as I heard about David, but all I got was a message that the phone had been disconnected. I knew something suspicious had happened, but I was whisked away so quickly that I could not get in touch with you.

"I ran into Grover Rankin once in the little village where I was hidden away. He was the one who sent the notes. He got out of the military. He could not stand it after David's team was done away with. I later looked him up under past military employees, and there is nothing on him. It is as if he never existed. I hate to think of what may have happened to Grover. He wanted very badly to tell you himself."

"Wow." David could hardly believe his ears.

"Yeah, wow!" the others echoed.

Jack, really not knowing what to make of it, said, "This makes me think that maybe I chose the wrong profession."

"Jack, what happened was done at the decree of the government, not the military. The military personnel were simply following orders. What was done to David and the other men was wrong, but it is no reason to give up on our country. Our government has its flaws, but it is still the best system in the world, and I've seen quite a few."

Everyone around the table nodded in agreement.

Anne tried hard to control the waver in her voice as she said, "My prayer right now is that none of us becomes bitter over this. I am feeling a little bitter pang right now. Nathan, will you pray for us that we can handle this as God's children and realize that all things work to the good of those who love the Lord and are called according to His purpose?"

"Father God, right now in the name of Jesus, I pray for this wonderful family, as well as Mrs. Stennis, Jack, and me. Help us to remember the good things about David and realize that he lives on in his children and grandchildren. Help us to go from this place tonight with a determination to handle this truth about David's death as You would have us to handle this. You are a great God, and we love You so very, very much.

"Thank You for bringing me to this place, for crossing my path with Annie after all these years. Help them as they may go through a period of grief again after hearing the truth. Please help us to treat the truth with caution and use it for Your glory to advance Your kingdom. In the precious name of Jesus we pray. Amen."

"So be it," Anne murmured.

CHAPTER TWENTY-FIVE

Anne determined in her heart to do as Nathan had prayed, to treat the truth about David's death with caution and use it only to the glory of her God. She knew from the looks on her children's faces that it might take them a while to absorb it all. She prayed that they would be okay.

"Nathan, thank you so much for coming here and telling us about that fateful Easter Sunday that changed all our lives. What can we do to repay you?"

Anne hoped that God would bless this kind man for bringing a peace that she had longed for so many times over the years.

"Just stay in contact with me and let me know how everyone is doing – and whenever you think of me, please pray for me."

Nathan hoped to see the Starling family again and get to know more about them.

"Mom, we've got to get the boys home," David said. "Mister Parker, thank you so much for coming. Mary, you live closer to us than to Mom or Katherine. Can we drop you off?"

"No, thank you, I have my car. Anne, will you be okay?" Mary asked, as protective as ever.

"I'll be fine. I'll check in with everyone after I drop off Nathan at the hotel."

"Mom, I can ride with you," Katherine offered.

"No, no, you ride with Jack. Lieutenant, we are glad that you joined us. I hope this didn't scare you from coming around anymore."

"No, ma'am, it will take more than this to scare off this ol' boy. It was wonderful to see all of you again. I'll be very careful driving your daughter, and I'll stay until she checks in with you."

Jack's manners scored him multiple brownie points with Anne and David.

Everyone shook hands with Nathan and thanked him again for coming to share his story with them.

"Anne, I'm going to take a taxi," he said. "You are very well known here, and I don't want anyone to see you pulling out of a hotel driveway at night. I have something that I want to give you. When Marilyn and I married, David gave me a pocket watch that had belonged to one of his uncles. I want you to take it, and when the time is right, give it to David the Second. I also brought a little something for you."

Nathan pulled the pocket watch and a small velvet box from his coat pocket.

Anne's hands trembled as she took the items from him. She opened the tiny box and almost cried. The box held a small pin with a rocket on it. Anne recognized the inscribed date: *1959*. David had begun work on the Apollo program that year. The first Apollo did not launch until after his death, but the designs had begun much earlier.

"Not long ago I was rummaging through an old storage room looking for some paperwork, and I ran across this." Nathan tried to maintain his composure as he spoke. "These pins were given to the men when they finished working on projects. I didn't know if David ever got one, and I thought you would like to have it."

"I have several items but nothing like this. I will wear it with pride, and when the time is right, I will give the pocket watch to David and the pin to Katherine. Thank you so much, Nathan. It has been good seeing you. I hope you will visit again. You are a part of this family now, and we expect to see family members on a regular basis."

"I have enjoyed it too. It was very emotional for all of us, but now maybe we will have peace. David was a fine man, and he would be very proud of you and of your two wonderful children. Annie, I know we were planning to have breakfast in the morning, but let's do it another time. I want you to rest tomorrow, and I can go to the base early and maybe they can give me an earlier flight. I want us to remember each other all dressed up, sitting in this fancy restaurant. I think it is fitting. We can go our separate ways for now and take time to absorb all of this information. Then I will come back and visit on a more carefree note. This trip is for David; the next one will be for me."

"You are a fine friend, Nathan Parker. Thank you so much for coming. Call us when you get home and let us know how you are doing. I agree, this is a fine ending for this meeting. God bless you, dear friend."

Annie touched Nathan's cheek as she said goodnight. Then she was gone.

Nathan called a cab and sat in the lobby. He bowed his head and thanked the Lord for allowing him to come and meet with the Starlings.

Anne made it home safely and, before going to bed, called each of her children and Mary, to let them know that she was in for the evening. Then she lay in bed wide-awake, for a long time, lost in her thoughts.

She thought of her dear husband and how dreadful his last moments on this earth must have been. She knew that he was a fine Christian man, and that he was at home with the Lord. She thought of her children and echoed Nathan's prayer that they would all handle the truth with caution. She thought of Mary and how faithful she and Webb had been to all of them. She thought of dear, sweet Nathan and how relieved he must feel to have gotten the truth about David's death off his chest.

She drifted off to sleep with a thankful heart.

Chapter Twenty-Six

THE next morning Nathan took a cab to the base, but on the way, he stopped at a florist and made a couple of purchases. He gave the cab driver an address, and they headed to the cemetery that Anne had pointed out on the driving tour the day before.

The cab driver drove into the cemetery, where Nathan got out and walked over to his friend's grave. On it, he placed a white floral arrangement complete with tiny flags. He stood over the grave, prayed for David's family, and then saluted his friend before returning to the cab. He knew that as soon as the florist delivered his other purchase, his work for this visit would be finished.

As the cab moved toward the base, Nathan pulled a calendar out of his briefcase and began to plan his next visit.

At about 2:00 in the afternoon, a delivery van pulled up to Anne Starling's home. Her doorbell rang, and when Anne came to the door, no one was there. The delivery van was pulling out of sight.

There was an arrangement of beautiful yellow roses, interspersed with white daisies, just like the ones used in her wedding, sitting on the steps. The simple note attached read, *For Annie*, and in the lower left-hand corner was the eagle signal, *IS4031*.

Knowing that the flowers were from Nathan, Anne felt like a schoolgirl. She was thankful that Nathan had come their way, and she looked forward to seeing him again.

Nathan got to the base and almost walked into Jack Hancock. Jack saluted the superior officer and Nathan 'at-eased' him quickly. Nathan told Jack that he had to tie up some loose ends and then was headed home. "I did put flowers on David's grave and sent a bouquet to Annie. I did not get to attend the funeral, and I have wanted to pay proper respect all these years. This is a bit of closure for me."

Jack looked like he wanted to ask Nathan a question as he shuffled uncomfortably from side to side. Nathan asked the younger man what was on his mind. "Well, you mentioned sending flowers and I have been thinking about…well, you know." Jack's voice trailed off and he suddenly seemed like a shy schoolboy rather than the confident military officer that Nathan had met last night.

Nathan grinned and said, "Send the lovely red-haired lady a big bouquet. I would start with something simple like daisies. After a few more dates, then send some serious flowers like red roses. She is a great gal with a wonderful family. From what I saw last night, she is definitely interested in you."

"Do you really think so? I have been wondering if I even have a chance with her." Jack was still shuffling from side to side like a nervous junior high boy.

Nathan slapped him on the back and said, "Man, you have a great chance. You are a great catch yourself; a fine military man with a wonderful career ahead of you. You and Katherine share the same beliefs; the rest is small stuff that can be worked out as you go along. Listen to me, Jack. If you care for her, do not let her get away. I was interested in a wonderful lady several years ago, but I let old memories, work, and other stuff keep me from committing to her. She went on and found someone else and, he snapped her up. Do not let that happen to you. Give it some time, and the two of you have fun. However, keep in mind that this could be it!"

Jack shook Nathan's hand and thanked him for the advice. As Nathan walked away, he saw Jack taking out his cell phone. He smiled and hoped that Jack was calling information for the number of the local florist.

As Katherine was getting ready to leave work, a delivery van pulled into the parking lot. She saw the guy get out with a bouquet of pink daisies. Her mom had called and told her that Nathan had sent her a bouquet, so she wondered if he had sent the flowers, as well. It did not seem likely, and the flowers might be for another staff member.

The delivery guy came in and said, "I have a delivery for Katherine Starling."

"That's me.' Katherine admired the pretty arrangement as she signed for it.

Mary and Michelle were grinning from ear to ear and Michelle said, "Well, don't keep us in suspense."

Katherine turned the card over and for Mary and Michelle's sake; she read what it said, "Flowers for a beautiful Lady, Jack."

The ladies said, "awe" in unison, and Katherine playfully shushed them. She headed toward the firm's front door with a renewed confidence. However, when she passed her dad's portrait, she thought of all that her mom had gone through. Was she willing to risk being involved with a military man? Was he serious about her, or did he send flowers to lots of women? Well, time would tell, but if any guy was worth a risk, certainly it was Jack Hancock.

Made in United States
Orlando, FL
11 November 2021